A MAP OF KEX'S FACE

A Map of Kex's Face

ROBIN WYATT DUNN

Published by
JOHN OTT

San Diego

This book was made possible through the efforts of our *Homo Erectus* ancestors, who left Africa in search of interesting adventures, and told us all about them.

Cover art by Barbara Sobczyńska

ISBN 978-1-940830-04-9

Library of Congress Control Number: 2014951558

Learn more about the author at www.robindunn.com

for Martin

It is not down in any map; true places never are.

— Herman Melville

A woman knows the face of the man she loves as a sailor knows the open sea.

— Honore de Balzac

How does one begin to map a face?

How does one begin to map anything? You begin with a scale.

The traditional map renders three-dimensional space into a two-dimensional diagram, rendering the Earth as a bird might see it, where every mile is reduced to an inch.

In four dimensions, one must also allow for time to make its headway into the map, so that one develops an appreciation for the changing nature of landscape, and of history. Four dimensional maps established the reputation of our Department of Cartography, here at Eidon.

I first became interested in faces when I was a student. They're so interesting, aren't they? These windows to the soul.

If the Earth, and all its rivers and forests and roads and mountains, are the windows to the body … ah, but my metaphor is not right. I believe this may be part of the problem.

You see, I am not sure, even now, that a face can be mapped. We may not yet possess the right cognitive tools. Still, I am trying. The first cartographers, especially in the Islamic World, were hated; despised. Such diagrams did not represent the elegant and complex relationships between men and god that built the Islamic Caliphates, some men cried then. And they were right. Maps are simplifications, designed to help us forget certain things, in order to focus on others. Maps do our thinking for us, you see. They are shortcuts.

Nothing wrong with shortcuts, as long as you have a reasonably good idea why you are making them.

Why then, did I start to map Kex's face?

I love him. There is that reason. Though we are no longer lovers.

Perhaps there is no other reason.

In Class:

"You see this region here?" I pointed at Kex's left cheekbone on the diagram I'd drawn on the board.

"In isolation, we can assess its characteristics, much as we might assess the characteristics of the seven hills of Rome, or any historically important region. What are its characteristics?"

I glare at my graduate class, waiting.

Martin says, "It's a small hill, the cheekbone. It provides character for the face . . . but we're looking at it in isolation. It's almost toroidal, on its own, a rising arc. But what does it mean, professor, to pretend that the cheekbone isn't connected to a face?"

"This is what cartography is," I say. "Accenting some characteristics and ignoring others. Drawing some things and not others. Deciding where the map ends. In this way it is like consciousness, which is a phenomenon, a self, that is always deciding: what do I need to know, and what do I not need to know. So again, what does the cheekbone tell us, all on its own?"

"It's lonely," says Sahar.

"Yes," says Martin.

"If we see it in isolation, it's lonely, but we don't know why," Sahar says.

"Why is it lonely?" I ask.

"Because it's a rising plane and seems to invite lowlands, naturally, but the lowlands are not there, the cheek is not there, nor the eye socket. Just this hill, with nothing below it. It is lonely; like a language isolate, like the nation of Hungary, parachuted into the Carpathian Valley, without cousins or overlapping history, writing itself into being from scratch."

"But not quite from scratch," I say.

"Almost from scratch," says Martin. "Whatever was there before is also inaccessible, to the conscious mind, we can only imply it was there through reason, or through dream. Through the imagination. As we imagine this silly cheekbone of Kex's must have been something else before, before it was this."

"Good," I say. "But why draw the map at all? Don't we know Kex? What does this map accomplish? We know what the man looks like. We know he has cheekbones and that they have a particular shape. Why consider them, or any part of his face, any feature of a landscape, in isolation?"

Sahar rises suddenly and bares her breast to the class. Her face is stern, and watchful.

"In isolation," she says. "My breast is only a rising arc, only a hill with a summit. Its character derives, in large part, from its function as an organ. But since I have bared it, here, where there are others to see it, this breast is no longer possible to be seen in isolation; I am connected to it, and you are seeing it. You cannot consider the features of my breast without considering me, Sahar, and your own relationship to me."

She slipped her breast back into her blouse and sat back down. There was quiet for a moment.

4

I am afraid. Because I am remembering other reasons why I began to draw this map.

Book One: California

Chapter 1

The room is peaceful, warm-colored with mood lighting, a synthetic fireplace burning a synthetic log behind a courtesy screen; oddly-shaped plush chairs fill the room.

I have been so many men, so many to get me this far. But now I know I must dispense with that oldest version of myself. I must become a savage.

Around me, carefully placed televisions afford optimal views from a dozen angles, their muted sounds blending with a gentle institutional music, as nearby trainees discuss the week's gossip.

My wife is named Sasha. Her extraordinary calm soothes me.

Old music comes on the stereo, filling me with loss, and one of the arms of the building extrudes -- from the far wall, its claws shining in the mood lighting, its gears well-oiled, it shimmers, hovering, moving towards me across the business lounge.

It attaches to my chest and my head jerks back, my wife stands, her eyes wide and her lips pressed together; she holds my head as the arm works its business in my gut.

It is like Frank Sinatra, the singer on the airwaves, but he is a woman, black, filled with eternal sorrow. My wife turns my head to the side so I can vomit the sputum.

The arm disengages from my body and slides back across the room, satiated.

"California is a madhouse, isn't it, Sasha?" I ask.

"I need to get back to work," she says, and takes out her computer.

I cough, and lie back against my chair. The machinery in my intestines makes low whirring noises.

After a moment I sit back up and take out my screen, touching the keys to bring up the image of the map I've been studying.

Blue-black lines twist out from a knotted center, hundreds and hundreds of tendrils, I zoom in on the one region I know better than the others.

Sasha reaches out to hold my hand.

I touch the surface of my screen. Red blinking lights shimmer off the surfaces of the tendrils on the map, representing Eidon Academy in four dimensions.

I turn off the screen and squeeze Sasha's hand. She speaks into her microphone, recording.

I raise my hand to summon the waiter.

The waiter stands amidst the lobby, hovering over our chaise lounges.

"Yes, what can I get you?" he says.

"We'll have the shrimp."

"Sauce?"

"Red."

My screen is shimmering with low light; a phone call. The damned machine answers on its own.

"Roberto."

"Kex."

"Welcome back."

"Are you all right?" I ask.

"You ordered the shrimp."

"Sasha and I are busy right now, Kex. Can I come up for a visit in an hour?"

"Of course."

I take the batteries out of my screen to stop the damned thing from answering calls on its own.

"I have to take this in private," says Sasha.

"So soon?"

She looks at me with that hovering and obedient rage that made me fall in love with her and turns to go into one of the curtained booths. She likes to take important phone calls in the nude. I watch her go into the booth and draw the curtain. I can see her smooth calves as she removes her shoes. A moment later her dress slips around her ankles.

The waiter brings the shrimp.

I crunch into one of them without dipping it in the sauce, watching the fried crumbs spill onto my slacks. I wipe my greasy hands on my pants, making a sound in my throat.

California.

Chapter 2

I give the remaining shrimp to the homeless man sitting outside the business lounge.

"Please eat them," I say.

He shoos me away and I go inside, up the stairs, winding around the medieval staircase towards the penthouse.

Seven floors up I present my face to the alcove by a glass gate, a laser flashes over my right eye; the gate opens on smooth gears.

I walk around the corner, my steps loud on the marble. Kex sits with his back to me, looking out at the tightly manicured surfaces of the Academy campus below him. Perched above Kex's shoulder on the edge of the chaise-lounge, a small dog regards me with evil eyes.

"Kex," I say. He turns around in his seat, smiles at me.

"Roberto!"

He walks to greet me, the dog yapping and following him. We shake hands, I watch his eyes carefully; he looks disturbingly the same as the last time I saw him, three years ago.

"You haven't changed," I say.

"Neither have you," he says.

"You still keep your bar?" I ask.

"Of course." He smiles. "Whiskey?"

"Yes."

The gears in my stomach make a little wheezy noise, anticipating the alcohol.

Halfway through pouring the second drink Kex spills the bottle; it tips to the floor, I go to catch it before it all pours out. Kex presses his head to the fabric-covered wall, tilting his forehead back and forth against the quilting.

Outside the sun speeds up; we've lost an hour of daylight.

I down my drink. The dog has been yapping furiously. I aim a kick at it but it dodges, fleeing down the marble corridor.

Kex is making low moaning noises, rolling his forehead back and forth slowly, against the wall.

I take out my screen and put the batteries back in and zoom back in on the region of black snakes.

I've labeled one of the tendrils "Doors." I tickle it with my finger on the screen, resting against one of its shiny red ribosomes.

A door opens in the wall by Kex, a portal into blackness. I've forgotten my flashlight today and my battery power is declining rapidly; I won't have long inside.

I activate the light function on my screen and hold it in front of me like a cross, illuminating the dusty surfaces of the secret corridor. I go inside, breathing through my mouth; the air is foul.

 The party is up ahead; I remember it, but it's worse now.

I bang on the stone door; the party noises inside increase.

"Open up, goddamn it!"

Ha ha ah aha.

I can hear Kex groaning back in his penthouse; my light is beginning to dim.

"Please open!"

The wall clicks and slides open a notch. I turn off my screen, dig my fingers into the notch and pull.

The dancers and the jazz musicians stand at attention, their shiny black suits glimmering in the candlelight.

"You messed up again," I announce. "It's pathetic. Give me a jazz tune."

The cellist and the accordion player strike up a melancholy version of "Begin the Beguine" and I move to sit in Alice's lap, big homely Alice, soft in all the places that Sasha is hard, surrounded with Alice's familiar fragrance.

I announce to them, keeping time to the music:

"It isn't intervention, it isn't celebration, it isn't even sexual anymore . . . I don't know what to do. I have a job I have a life I have a lover I have my strife out on the moors inside my dreams . . . tell me is it true you thought me rueful when I came inside, because the joy was burning in me and I need to get it through, I need to shake it off and stew with all of you because you've got what I can never have: pull . . ."

"So sad, Roberto," Alice whispers in my ear. I lean back against her breasts, listening to the music.

The music speeds up and I know I have to go, but I don't want to. I get up and dance instead, and Alice joins me, shaking her bulk, her belly fat swaying and jiggling, her hair smooth and sexy like Janice Joplin.

I want to dance forever but the door is starting to close and I run for it, slipping through the gap, my shoe stuck in it as I slip through, I get my foot out and the wall crushes the leather; that was an expensive fucking shoe!

I hold my hands against the filthy walls of the secret corridor, stalking back towards the light.

The dog is sleeping on Kex's chest. It opens its eyes when I enter.

On impulse I pull out my screen and place it on the charging station by the bar, and next to the ribosome labeled "Doors" I write, "Dog."

The dog blinks.

I'm a cartographer. But my maps no longer bring a sense of control; they're making new things all the time, every day, my charts produce phenomena I cannot comprehend; I fear I'm dying.

Chapter 3

I'm making love to Sasha. Her svelte body curves around my awkward one, slick in my hands.

She tastes like pepper. I come inside her and I want to scream, I want to bash my head against the wall. She is angry.

I kiss her breast and get up to use the bathroom.

She activates her inhaler and takes some of the nitrous she's grown fond of these last months; some new DNA-laced flavor.

I turn on the shower and she comes to stand at the bathroom door, her eyes glazed from the drug, a wry smile on her lips.

"You really don't know who you are, do you?"

"Come in with me," I say.

I soap her long, lovely body in my hands.

- -

A storm has come in. I walk out into it, rainwater slicking my face, soaking my coat. Lightning strikes the clock tower and the rod glows. The hairs along my neck rise. I want to laugh but I hold it back; I just smile soft into the storm, watching the trainees run into their dormitories, chattering like birds, watching the flood control channels rise from the manicured lawns to guide the waters off the walkways. A crow flies overhead; I hear its cry.

I want some of that nitrous too but I have to work.

Under an awning by the women's dormitory I take out my freshly-charged screen and aim its camera at the plaza center. The program maps the pattern of the rainfall and generates a visual simulacrum for me in another window, twisted nightmarish beautiful like the tendrils and ribosomes, but bright red and spiky.

The rain is slowing down; I reach my hand out from cover of the awning and can see my hand is moving faster than the falling drops.

I activate the dictaphone and speak:

"This body, like a moon, a falling body in space, presents itself to our contemporary urban awareness as a gemstone to the loupe eyepiece of a jeweler, attentive to its graces and footnotes; we must do more, though, we must read it as the geomancer does or the tea-leaf reader, not to read the future but to know the present."

I shut off the dictaphone.

One of the trainees has noticed me, stroking the grains of water trapped in her shining hair out onto her palm, which she presents for my inspection; the water is shining.

"You shouldn't be out in this weather," I say.

"I can be out wherever I want."

Her body is taut and muscular. A narrow nose. Wide, startling eyes.

"Yes, of course you can. Would you like to see my notes?"

"Okay."

I show her the screen, zooming in on the red tangles of the rainfall patterns.

"What program is that?" she asks.

"You see here? That's the fountain in the square. With every drop that falls into it, the fountain releases energy into the air, in a flowing pattern like smoke from a chimney. That, more than the physical erosion of the mantelpieces and busts of heads of state, that energy release will ultimately demand the removal of this site of the Academy to another biome."

"It's pretty," she says.

We watch the blue iris-shaped growths of the simulacrum form bulbs on my screen which shatter into thin glass extrusions at precise geometric angles, coruscating, again, like the rainfall, but faster and in all directions at once.

"Come upstairs with me," she says.

I look at her.

"I need help with my biology experiment."

I laugh, despite myself, but her eyes are serious.

"All right," I say.

She waves her wrist in front of the door's scanner; she opens the door for me and I go inside the lobby. It is narrow and Victorian, with a huge gnarled oak banister leading to the sleeping floors.

I sign in with the guard, and follow the coed upstairs. At her floor, we turn down the hallway. Another young woman is standing outside of her room.

"I can't sleep," she says.

"Mirie, go to sleep," my coed says.

"What are you guys doing?"

"Her biology experiment . . ." I explain, and promptly receive a blow on my shoulder from the young woman.

"I can't sleep," Mirie says again.

"Why not?" I ask.

"Bad dreams."

"I have those," I say.

"Are we going to talk out here all night?" my coed says, looking me in the eye.

"No," I say, taking her hand, and guiding her down the hall.

She opens her door and I follow her into her room.

"I lucked out with my private room this year," she says. "Don't mind the pottery."

Cups, plates and teapots in various stages of glazing litter the floor.

"I work better in the nude," she says, stripping her clothes off and donning surgical gloves which she pulls out of a box on her bookshelf.

17

As I undo my belt, I notice the long low table at the far end of the room, set only a few inches off the floor, like a coffee table for cats.

Finely crafted wooden blocks, less than a centimeter thick, form an elaborate maze on the table.

I go to stand next to her and look down at the maze.

Little figures wind their way inside of it; three of them. Little people.

"Are they holograms?" I ask.

"Yes," she says. "But they're alive."

I run my hand through her hair; it is very soft. "What can I do to help?"

"I don't want you to touch me yet," she says. "I want you to get your computer and run some numbers for me."

I sigh and go back to fetch it, stepping carefully between the pots.

Lightning strikes outside again and the hairs on my neck rise, along with my prick, but I bend to get the screen and return to the maze, kneeling to turn the computer's metal eye upon the small prisoners inside the wooden maze, gratified that the young woman is looking at me.

"How do you want me to influence your subjects?" I ask.

"Speak to them, professor. While you map them."

Chapter 4

The Ambassador arrives next week. Chai-Murry, a dimension close to our own, normalized diplomatic relations with us last year but have yet to send an emissary. It's said that he, or she, will be coming soon, and a room has been reserved.

Sasha is working on her diorama, moving her exacto-knife like a shoemaker.

I want to bang my head against the window.

"I'm going out."

Everything smells fresh after the rain. The squirrels are plotting an elaborate prank; I watch their signals along the wall outside my building.

My tomatoes are starting to die; I can taste the slow death in the fruit I crush between my teeth.

The old woman sees the tomato seed spilling down my chin into my beard. I suck it back into my mouth.

She is standing under the balcony, watching the trees.

"Good morning," I say. She nods. I watch the trees with her.

The sky trembles with the coming heat; I feel like a boy again, ready to hunt for an ice cream cone, and a video game.

A dog nearby is panting, almost choking.

"Did you enjoy the storm?" I ask.

"No."

"You don't like storms?"

She gazes off at the trees again.

I feel like rolling in the grass, like a dog.

"Enjoy your day!" I call after the old lady. I walk down the sidewalk, a certain picture of a domestic urbane gentleman, mad and lonely and fruity, burned inside.

The day is terrifying to me. But I'm growing used to terror.

The crows have been watching closer and closer; I know they're learning my secrets and I don't mind. Perhaps I encourage it. They know my face well now; I hear them warn the others when I'm coming.

Once years ago I helped a wounded crow and so befriended the community, but it is possible I have made too much of my generosity that day, and should do more for the crows, though Sasha believes they are our enemies.

My friend is soaring over me.

I should call the coed; buy her coffee. But I don't want to be surrounded with adolescent angst today.

I watch the skyline, the hills in the distance, and the mountains behind them, very clear today, though clouds are moving in, high above, and sinking.

A plane is landing; I feel its breeze on my face as it passes over my head. My friend the crow has alit on the tree nearest me; he watches me with his cruel-kind eye.

I smile.

I take out my phone, and call Remy.

"What is it?" he says.

"Beautiful day."

"Roberto. Sorry. Things are happening over here."

"What things?"

"Tell you later!" He hangs up. My friend the crow takes off back into the sky.

I might as well as go see who was on the plane. I enjoy arrivals.

Last month I had been working on a sarcastic performance art piece titled "Eidon Academy: putting the anal back in analysis since 1983" but decided it was too juvenile for a professor of my stature. Only now I wish I had done it anyway; visitors always love a juicy gaffe.

They're stepping down from the gangway onto the tarmac as I pass through the fence, waving. One waves back, somewhat confused. The others glance my way briefly before heading into the shelter of the terminal.

- -

The jet rears and turns for takeoff. I skip over to the small terminal and shake a few hands.

It cheers me. I needed that.

Later, in the anteroom of Professor Bulbo's chambers, I look at his portrait which hangs outside his office: the dignified moustache, the stovepipe hat at the jaunty angle, and the gemstone, set above his brow; his third eye.

I knock.

"Come in." Professor Bulbo's deep voice. I enter, and see the twinkle in his eye, and know he has been playing with the rats again. I can almost hear their squeaks.

"Jack."

"Roberto."

"I need your help."

"A drink?"

I sit and watch him pour. The sherry smells terrible but tastes quite good. The glasses are dirty.

"You've been expanding your maps," Bulbo says.

"Yes."

"Incredible work."

"I need to see your rats," I say.

"My rats?"

"Yes."

"They're not my rats."

"Your friends, I mean. The rats. I need to see them."

"Whatever for?" He leans back in his chair with a humorous sneer.

"I need their help."

- -

It is dark already. I have missed the day. The clouds are coming back.
The plaza expands slowly, tied to the tectonics beneath us. The stones spread carefully between the tufts of native grasses. At their center, the fountain and its bust of Enrico Fermi, smoking a corncob.

I missed the sunset. I want to bathe in the fountain. I remove my clothes. The water is delicious.

Cold, but so delicious.

A guard arrives with a flashlight. My damned luck! I start to climb out of the fountain but see his beam wave towards me and decide it is better to remain within.

He stands by the fountain, shining the light in my face.

I give him the finger. He raises the flashlight, as though to strike me with it, and I swim back, to the other side of Enrico Fermi and he stalks around the fountain, snarling. I swim back again, to the other side, a bizarre adolescent game of tag. I'm it.

No, he's it.

"I'm an employee of the Academy!" I shout, but it does no good. The guard is climbing into the fountain, full in uniform, his pants soaked, his teeth shining in the starlight, and I flee naked over the stones, back to my wife.

- -

I'm pounding on our apartment door in the nude. One of my neighbors opens her apartment door a crack, quickly shuts it.

My wife opens the door and I embrace her, shivering. I kiss her lips. She takes off her robe and presses her warm skin to my goosebumps.

I must find the rats.

I am tangled in my wife's body for hours, and then it is light.

Chapter 5: The Emissary

They are hanging out the Chai-Murry bunting, like tinsel only in more dimensions; it refracts light at bizarre angles. It's said the emissary will be contented with such decoration.

Over by the football field I can see Professor Bulbo, stroking the bare skull of the iron bust of Richard Chanwich, the Academy's founder. He is deep in thought.

Where would he hide the rats?

I dare not dig a thousand holes over our carefully manicured campus.

A young woman approaches me. It's Mirie, my coed's neighbor.

"Mirie!"

"Professor."

"Mirie, have you seen the rats?"

"No, professor." She wipes hair out of her eyes; she's been sweating.

"Hot one, isn't it?" I say.

"Not really."

I can see Bulbo putting on his running shoes. The bust of the founder seems to levitate in this heat, as though to float above and watch Bulbo's circumambulations.

"Shall I buy you a lemonade?" I ask.

"Let me buy you a lemonade," Mirie says.

"Sold."

We walk down to the lake, where Pablo keeps his ice bucket.

Pablo grins as we approach.

She pays him with her chits, and Pablo sighs. He stuffs the cardboard into his pocket and hands us our drinks. Perhaps the rats are around the lake today. They could be anywhere. It is growing so hot!

"Do you know Professor Bulbo?" I ask.

"No."

"Haven't you seen him?"

"No."

"Thank you for the lemonade," I say.

"Mmm."

"It's getting hot."

Back at the plaza I can hear the Door warming up; the emissary.

"He's coming," says Mirie. I'm reminded suddenly of my coed's lithe body, like a dancer's. Mirie is portly by comparison, but so solicitous.

"We should go greet him," I say, but I don't have the energy.

"It might be a her," says Mirie, sounding as bored as I am.

"True."

"Such a sexist, Professor."

"I know."

She stops and looks at me. I sip my frozen lemonade.

She starts to say something but stops.

"I have to go, professor," she says.

"Shall I walk you?"

"No. Goodbye."

"Bye."

I watch her generous ass as she moves away. I'm sweating. One of the rats emerges from the lake.

I bend immediately to greet it, holding out my hand. It watches my fingers.

I watch its eyes. Its nose twitches.

I twiddle my fingers. The rat hisses.

Another one is coming out of the lake. It shakes its wet fur, like a dog. Its eyes are large, and insane. Like mine.

"I am here on Bulbo's behalf," I find myself saying. One of the rats' ears bend back, like an angry cat's. The other, the crazy one, comes closer to me, listening.

"The squirrels sent me," I try again. One of the rats makes a warbling sound.

I need a breath; I stand and walk down the lakeshore, the rats twitter behind me. I want to skip, and almost do, the energy in me's a killer, it's rambunctious and afraid, it's a cord, tying me to an energy field I cannot see, like Chai-Murry, a dimension so close to our own you can almost touch it . . .

I run around the lake. In my inappropriate running clothes, my cloak too heavy and too wet, my beard chafing my face, the sun blinding white.

- -

By the time I get back to my apartment I see the Emissary's already arrived; the provosts and the chancellor are making the ceremonial motions in the plaza, presenting the Emissary with scrolls and gift baskets, wine, cheese, personal arms. A small gold Derringer glitters in the light; I doubt it's functional, but it's pretty. I go up the apartment stairs and throw my stinking clothes by the bathroom door and leap into the shower, singing,

It's a bawdy devil
Who took me away
It's a bawdy devil
Who's come and said to me,
Go home,
Go home, wanderer,
Go home . . .

I'm to sing in the choir for the Emissary this evening. I enjoy singing but prefer the impromptu variety.

Outside I see echoes of my coed's holograms wandering the campus, their mouths stretched in rictus, trotting over the stones like gargoyles with clipped wings.

I dry off and put on my best medieval wear. The red floppy hat hang over my right eye; I clasp my gold scepter in my left hand, a vestige of when the scholars would beat the townspeople into submission in the street, to keep bread prices low.

Back outside, my coed sees me and matches my eyes with a long, slow look, I feel I'm falling; I can't look away. She looks away first and I continue on towards the ceremony, swinging my scepter like a billy club in my hand, watching the light flicker off it.

"Roberto," says Professor Bulbo.

"Jack," I say.

"Shall we?"

We join hands and begin the *deus ex theologium*, god from the god-word, the invocation of our temporary lease on this earth, singing in the traveler and his retinue, in obedience to our ancestors' mores, in obedience to our own.

I'm laughing amidst the choral sound; my second tenor is scratchy, I've been drinking too much.

We're inside the altar room, burning some of the heretical texts we copy every year, a reminder of the quantum physicists who denied our Door was possible.

I watch the ash swirl into the air and smile; science is so funny. Always changing.

The Emissary is a large man, corpulent even. He has an unnerving smile, and his English is very strange; it sounds almost like Frisian. But it isn't Frisian. It's Chai-Murrian.

I'm starting to fall asleep; Bulbo elbows me in the ribs. I straighten my hat and raise my scepter in salute after the Emissary smears the ash on his face.

I think I need a vacation. But my research is finally starting to go well. And now I have three classes to teach.

"He's a large one, isn't he?" I ask Bulbo, watching the Emissary. Bulbo grins.

Chapter 6

Something has gone amiss, but I'm not sure what. My mood is spoiled, and I wish . . .

Well.

Nothing for it now but to keep working, try to figure out what's happened.

Kex is on vacation. The semester has begun. I grow old, I wear my trousers rolled, but what now?

I'm studying the fountain, catching the light off the water patterns and marking their frequencies on my map. Time has been very regular; synchronicity returned to normal, since the Emissary's visit. Perhaps the door requires temporal jumps in preparation for its opening but the data are not consistent.

I put on music which always helps me in my studies. The brain implant screens were made available last year but I find them distracting; I prefer coprocessors to remain external to my skull.

- -

I'm running, which helps me think. One of my trainees asked me, "Why did you become a professor?" Well, I needed to make a living. And that's what I told the trainee. But I should have said something else. I should have said . . . I don't know.

Something inspiring.

The light is sliding off the water like mist, tendrils and flakes of light, coiled round one another, like ribosomes on my tendrilled map, twisting themselves into the air. The drums coming from campus announce the hours, slow and steady, an African variation on medieval church bells. California; I love you, but what are you doing to me?

We live in an imaginary land. An island—

What is the light and what is my mind; I feel it working in me. The light makes me light on my feet, light-headed, and yet light has a weight, every photon, bearing down on my flesh, marking my retinae and spine with their slow embrace.

I've kept the quantum pistol in my bag; it fires radio-frequency-transmitting bullets. I load a round, aim at the center of the lake, and fire. The concussion in my hand is very satisfying; I feel I can bring down a buffalo. I will bring the woman buffalo steak tonight.

I open my screen and map the course of the bullet down into the lake mud deeper into the crust, penetrating 5,000 feet a second, slowing, slowing . . . it will stop before it reaches the mantle.

The pistol is an unstable device but only at night; in darkness it can achieve self-awareness and so I keep it in a well-lit safe, the size of a shoe box, which is where I put it now.

It's not my job to suss out Kex's politics, to tell the man who should he become, or even what I may believe about who he's been; who he is. Yet I find I must do exactly that, to complete my map. All maps are political documents, I suppose.

The old woman is back, staring at the trees. I know she's a friend of the crows, too. But we've never spoken of it.

As I pass her, she calls to me:

"Professor!"

"Good afternoon."

"Professor, have you ever been to Chai-Murry?"

"Why, no. I don't believe such transits are permitted. I'm curious though. Are you curious?"

She glances at me but keeps looking at the trees.

"Professor, I've been to Chai-Murry."

"Oh?"

"Do you believe me?"

"No, I don't."

She smiles a little.

"Ten years ago," she says.

"The gate has only been opened for two years, madame."

"I've lived here a long time, professor. Don't you think I know more about this place than you?"

"How did you go, then?"

"In a dream."

"I see. You dreamed it. I myself am fond of dreams."

"It wasn't a dream. I went there *in a dream.*"

"How nice for you. I'm afraid I have a class to teach. Perhaps you'll tell me about your dream another time?"

She nods, and smiles a thin smile.

Almost as an afterthought, I call after her as I leave: "What news from the crows?"

"They've been talking about you," she says.

Of course Eidon Academy has a special relationship with dreams; mainly of the American kind. But the kind that happen while asleep, I find I can't understand.

- -

Some of the military's planes have been doing an exercise; a smattering of trainees are out in protest.

Their signs catch the light and I feel the urge to take out my computer to scan the wavelengths but I restrain myself; I should enjoy the political moment.

One sign says "Planes are wrong," which makes me want to burst out laughing, so I go and stand next to that guy, absorbing his strong energy. The picketers stand beneath the passing planes, like palms against the ocean, waiting for the wave to break.

I am thinking of my wife, and listening to the engines of the plane growl over us, shooting the military colored streamers in their wake, turning the sky black and yellow and pink. Her sexuality is like my cloak, shelter from the sky, terrible and warm and lightning.

One of the protestors has begun to cry, and I help him hold up his sign.

He continues to stand there, crying, half-holding up his sign, long minutes after the rest have departed, hating the planes with all his might. I give him a kiss on his cheek and lay the sign down on the grass and call my wife on my phone:

"Take off all your clothes."

Chapter 7: Fired

I'm lying in bed; my wife is out of town, which I hate. Kex calls me on the phone and I sit up in bed, so I sound halfway serious; I should be in the library working.

"Roberto."

"Kex."

"What's been happening."

"The Ambassador is here. The Emissary."

"I know. What's he been doing?"

"I don't know. The Chancellor has been keeping him to himself."

"I want you to photograph the Emissary."

"Yes?"

"Yes."

"Can you be more specific?"

"No."

"Great."

"I really need you help on this one, Roberto. I won't be back for another week."

"Where are you anyway?"

"Chai-Murry."

"Really."

"Goodbye, Roberto. Get those pictures."

"Roger. Arrivaderci."

"It will be good for both of us, Rob."

I want to go back to sleep. But I get into the shower and put on clothes and walk downstairs with my screen.

Maybe I should just invite the Emissary for a photography session! The direct approach works sometimes.

I head over to the Administration building.

It's coming, but . . . I can't tell you that yet.

Just pretend it isn't coming.

That's what I do. Each time I remember what I did.

- -

I mean, what do you got babe?

What do you got?

Was it something that you saw, or something that you felt?

Something that made me move, that made you run?

Was it the sun or the earth that moved you over these hills
to the border of our central park empire, burgeoning to
throw our streamers over some cliff we can't see--

I know you--

I know what you want, woman: everything.

I've been fired.

Cascading arrays of lightning blue and green wreathe round my arms and hands as I disconnect from the systems arrays employed within the university my body is the starter of a system of engines but we have many starters and I must be re-encoded. They would prefer I leave but I'm here, under the same sky, the same "sheltering" sky, but a different sky now too, no longer as much mine, no longer as great a threat. I am a free man, a free mason, a working man without work, an academic without an academy.

My wife has thrown me out.

I sit under the tree under the light rain, the coruscating energy of the university programming beginning to dissipate; most of the locks have been changed.

Kex is nowhere to be found. The chancellor has pulled a coup. I'm on the outs. *Persona non grata.*

But I still have my screen.

And I still have my gut.

I had slipped into the vestibule with my camera mode activated; they were ready for me. Never even got off a shot. Not even a formality. Four years of work.

Anyway. It's starting to rain in earnest. I put on my hood.

My coed sits down next to me. She puts her arm around my shoulders. Invites me to her bed. In the dorm.

What must I do.

\- -

Homelessness is, in a perverse way, like coming home. Our home is the trees, you know, and when we are homeless and have much less protection but remain in the human community, at the mercy of our fellow man at last, we come home to our home in the trees.

I sit in the business lounge surrounded by the eager beaver trainees. Their authority derives from a separate administration here on our campus, a secular one. If they are the king's and we are God's (though I am no longer included), then it makes sense that they are so close and I am so far away.

I am homeless, but perhaps I always was.

I sit in the business lounge. (Emotion flows over the room like the bad music, inescapable, each to each, cheek to cheek). Wandering around campus and watching my colleagues pretend they do not know me, pounding on my apartment's door, sleeping under the tree, watching the raindrops.

Bulbo gave me some croissants, and a towel. I have dried my face.

I am in the business lounge. But what is its business? I could stand and shout, but security would come, soon enough. The lounge's real security are the young trainees, bright and young and innocent, their purses filled with money, with business plans.

The electric glow of my mind enacts some frequency unknown to me, I am betrayed, by myself...

Help me. Will you?

Chapter 8: The Library

I still have my screen. And in the library I can recharge it. Some of my former trainees have been feeding me; their parents buy them too many meal plans.

I call Kex.

"The party you have called is unavailable. Press one for a holographic summons."

I press one.

"The holographic summons is unavailable. Thank you . . . for calling . . ."

I need Kex. He knows what this means. Bulbo won't say. My wife hates me. My sudden unemployment has confirmed her worst suspicions; I am a failure.

I should kill myself. Some part of me feels that the beauty of our country, this light, this beautiful California light, is the suicide. It comes here to die, to wash over us, finally complete.

In the library I can work. On my project. The lounge chairs here aren't like the business lounge; the lighting is all natural, from large windows, with a few careful sconces here and there. The voices of young trainees filter up from the rotunda below . . .

I should tell you just a little about our country. We've broken off. We are afloat upon the ocean. A magical isle. Of course this is only a tale we tell, the magic. The army keeps us safe, though mostly it is our propaganda . . .

But that is not really about our country, you see. You've seen it, I know. On your screen. Our light, you see, is very important, it has a quality which exists nowhere else. It is the magic. It is what I am studying.

I am dreaming of my wife's body. Daydreaming. I feel I will never meet another person again.

- -

The Ambassador made an announcement today, in Chai-Murrian, with simultaneous translation.

He stood under the eaves of the palms, his arms raised in benediction, his girth impressive beneath his white robes. He said:

"These days are fragrant with desire, and I enable them to be what we have needed, what is most needed, our awareness. These are things which we would discuss with you, if you would have us. So many things have come to pass since we became acquainted, so many strange coincidences and acts, so many beautiful flowerings of lurid powers and knife fights taking hold in the mind . . . I am the attachment of my people, I bring a new way for your usefulness; it is a smile but it is also a message, and the message is: change. Change now!"

Polite applause. Some camera flashes. The Ambassador lowers his arms and straightens his robes. I slink back to the library, where a trainee acquaintance awaits me, holding a small bottle of whiskey.

I taste it from the black bottle and want to vomit but choke it off. I smile at my drinking companion. It's going to be a long night.

42

As long as I leave at 2 a.m. while the library is being cleaned, they'll let me back in 3:30am so I can usually get some good hours of sleep in on a couch before the trainees return in the morning.

My gut needs maintenance today and I have made time to visit the machine in the basement, by the computer room. I hold the wall as the metal arm twists in me, like a woman leaning over for a man, presenting myself for the deed.

\- -

I am nude, watching the wave, my coed sits beside me, sipping her martini. I mark their movements on my screen. I feel for them, though it is wrong. I know that empathy is a destructive force as regards holograms. Too much empathy would give them power over us. I know that, but I feel for them anyway. They are trapped, and I have the power to free them . . .

It seems I was fired for finally becoming too political. It was only a photograph. But it was unauthorized. What does this mean?

I need to get my job back.

"Pay attention!" My beautiful coed nudges me in the ribs.

I realize it now. A bureaucratic error! There was something wrong with the translation! I remember, the Ambassador saw me, and he looked amused, and he said something to the chancellor, which was translated . . .

I remember, right before they took my camera. He was amused.

"I need to learn some Chai-Murrian," I say to my co-ed.

"Are we done working?" she says.

"I'm sorry. Yes."

She kisses me, and I hold her breast in my hand. I move next to her, and reach my hand around her waist. She kisses me back, angrily, tasting of salt.

- -

I thought things would be different. The light over campus is a breeze over my life; this my research, my life. I am a vessel. (And a vassal). But what is the knowledge I contain?

Storms shatter the sky, more every month. The colors that have come have never been seen before. I'm sinking into it, a dangerous thing, because of gravity. We are sinking in.

I'm crying. My coed throws me out. Too emotional. Where is the strong man she knew?

I'm coming to understand something. I'm coming to it. These colors, my god.

Over the east. Like a sunrise on crack, scraping like an amoeba, rosy-fingered dawn octopi, seething over the sky.

I call my wife.

"Honey."

She says nothing.

"Honey I need you."

Nothing.

"You remember that time we found that twenty dollar bill in my jeans pocket? When we first moved in together and were broke."

"Oh my God," she says.

"You remember that?"

"You're quoting that fucking Tom Cruise movie."

"I know."

I'm getting soaked.

"Where are you?" she says.

"I'm outside."

"Come up," she says. I'm shivering; we make love. Under the thunder outside, under her body. I come inside her and when I fall asleep after I come inside the dream that I've been looking for, the sketch of the color.

- -

Kex is standing over me. I'm lying on my wife's favorite white faux-bear rug. I'm nude, and I grab the bear head and put it over my crotch. Now Kex is looking down into two faces, me and the fake bear.

"Get dressed. The Chancellor wants to see you," says Kex.

"He does?"

"Mm-hmm."

45

"Okay."

I get dressed and make the coffee for Kex in my kitchen, although I suppose it might not be my kitchen now. We sip it and watch the rain outside through my window, not speaking. Just smelling the coffee and the rain.

- -

The Chancellor is waiting in the library, under the chandelier.

The Chancellor is waiting, waiting for the chandelier to fall. We're all waiting for it, watching it tremble from the ceiling.

On the Chancellor's head the holy crown is resting. In his hand rests the scepter and I hold my own small one, club of right and blood, gold and iron.

Kex holds my hand. I have shaved. I wear my robes.

The thunder is increasing. I see outside, the blue lightning.

The library is bright, so bright.

"You've come, Roberto."

"Yes, Chancellor. Allow me to apologize for my behavior—"

"That won't be necessary, Roberto."

"You acknowledge me?"

"I do. Though not all are in agreement. For now, I act alone."

"No one is with you?"

"Not yet."

The Chancellor smiles, the smile rippling over his broad face. The blue lightning plays with the bright incandescents, licking the edges of the gold fixtures like careful caterpillars, seeking food.

"How can I help you, Chancellor."

"Roberto," says the Chancellor, raising his scepter under the trembling chandelier. "I pronounce you my successor."

"Sir, I have no interest in administration—"

"Neither did I. It is a duty. In the faculties of university, the ministers are its arms. We climb. We row. We swing. We embrace. Will you embrace, me brother?"

"Yes, Chancellor."

Kex rests his hand on my shoulder. And I inhale the heady perfume of the Chancellor's flesh, and feel the jiggle of his belly, as he squeezes me in his broad arms.

The chandelier falls.

And lightning fills the room.

I who have become many men in my life became then both murderer and savior, as I dove, abandoning my friend the Chancellor, colliding with Kex as the lights went out.

The choir sang. They'll sing through anything; they're a recording.

The Chancellor lies buried beneath the chandelier, dead.

"Kex!" I say.

The lightning is increasing. And the thunder, filling my head. A window shatters, the wind soars in.

I saw Kex drag the bloodied chandelier off the Chancellor's body, and I watched him tug the holy crown from off his head, and watched him walk to me, and plop the metal circle onto my sweating brow.

"Your maps have done this, Roberto. These terrible maps of yours. Let's get out of here before we're drowned."

I called the police as we left the library, running through the lightning to the dormitory. I buzzed my coed, and screamed into her building's phone-box:

"Let us in! Please!"

She rings us up.

The dormitory is one of the strongest buildings on campus; it can endure a small nuclear detonation. Our trainees are our lifeblood.

Chapter 9: The Dormitory

Outside my friend the crow is flapping in the rain, pecking at the window. I take a hit from the bong and pass it, then go to the window and open it.

The trainees shout as I let in the cold, but they admire my friend, as he shakes the water from his feathers.

"Nevermore!" jokes one of the first-years.

"It's a crow, not a raven," I say, and reach into my pocket for some of the salami slices I keep for him. I tear off a piece and toss it to him and he snatches it up and swallows it, watching me, watching the window, watching us stoners.

Kex takes a hit from the bong.

"Chai-Murry is like nothing you've ever seen," he says, letting the marijuana smoke out of his mouth in a long low stream, "like nothing you've even dreamt."

"What did you do, Kex?" I say, feeding my friend another salami slice.

"I made arrangements."

"You did it all on your own, didn't you?"

"Yes."

"You could be arrested. Tortured even. God knows."

"I could but I won't be. I've ensured our future, Roberto. I've tied us tighter than we've ever been, to Chai-Murry. Your research can continue!"

I scratch my beard, and decline another round of the bong. My coed watches me with her dark hawk eyes, saying nothing.

"But I'm Chancellor now."

- -

Chancellor, chancellor. Keeper of the barrier, is what the word means, literally. But our barrier is gone.

- -

But that's wrong. The barrier is not gone, it merely changes.

I've begged my coed to assist me further, promising I will return the favor. I can't be without her, not now.

She holds her own screen, monitoring me, as I monitor the door to Chai Murry.

"What are you reading?" I ask.

"Some Flaubert. Marx. A little Jules Verne . . ."

"What are you reading on your screen!" I glare at her.

She smiles. "You're on fire, man. You're glowing."

"That's okay. It'd be worse if I wasn't glowing at this point," I say.

I edge closer to the door. "How about now?"

My energy is a fever. Our zeitgeist just hit a new frequency.

"Did you see that spike, Michelle?" (That's my coed's name. But I didn't want to tell you. Things are changing . . .)

"I think you should edge AWAY FROM THE DOOR, Professor . . ."

I do as she says.

And it shoots a big bullet of light up into the sky, over our faces.

I lean over her face and whisper in her ear:

"I don't think these phenomena have anything to do with what I'm studying."

"Why not, professor?"

"Even if they do, it's on a level beyond one I can understand with my equipment. All these signals are completely anomalous. They don't respond to any of the algorithms I've been using."

"Maybe your algorithms are wrong . . ."

I slip down over her mouth and suck on her lower lip. Blue tendrils of fire play along her cheekbones from the air.

"I don't think so, but it's possible. No, I think that I'm functioning on the equivalent of Newtonian physics, and the door is on another wavelength entirely. I'm going to have simply try to ignore it for my study."

"That's awkward . . ."

"Come on, let's get some lunch."

\- \-

She grouches over her tuna sandwich like a diva, picking at flaws in the toasting of the bread, examining every scrap of fish before closing her sandwich again and taking another bite.

She's so young.

"I'm Chancellor now. It doesn't feel quite real."

"The title is related to the verb cancel. It has an interesting etymology," she says.

"Keeper of the barrier."

"Are you going to keep my barrier? Or are you going to pimp me out?"

"I'm not really hard up for cash."

"Oh no?"

"Not yet."

"What about your wife?"

"What about her?"

The sun is mine; I'm the sun god. It is yours too, of course. All of ours. But especially mine, when I study it. The pathetic fallacy is a misnomer; I believe now in the fallacy fallacy, that it is fallacious to believe in fallacies. The universe knows we're here.

It shines over my shoulder, illuminating the lake. Contractors have begun to repair the hole in the library, erecting scaffolding and programming the droids. One of the droids, freshly activated, looks over at me with its cool red eyes before beginning its work.

"I need to hobnob. I'm a goddamned politician now."

"Bye sweetheart."

I stroke her hair, and leave her, hands in my pockets, a modern man in a modern city, on the floating isle of California, free of responsibility, burdened with a new and heavy academic title, keeper of the keep, a goddamned recursive business! Keeping and being kept . . .

My wife is watching me from the balcony. I wave. She watches me.

The Door did not implode as feared; I've allowed the Warning Level on the dormitories and outbuildings to be reduced to yellow.

Chancellors are a kind of judge; what judges do is separate. The innocent from the guilty. Nobility from commons. Real from imagined.

The map fills my mind like a cauldron fills with water and with love, frog legs and wine, the spirit of small gods mumbling to one another, enacting safeguards and miniature maelstroms in the bubbling of a recipe unknown even to me, the container of it, I'm like Johnny Mnemonic, courier for some ones and zeroes I can never open . . .

I call Kex.

"I need a drink, Kex."

"Come on up."

The dog is nowhere to be seen, thank God. I fucking hate
that goddamned dog.

Chapter 10

What began as a map of Kex's face became a map of campus, and has since expanded to include a map of its denizens and concomitant energy forces . . . a face is a kind of map, a map of the soul.

"I'm almost out of whiskey," Kex says.

"That is a California tragedy."

"The Chemistry labs can whip up a still in a jiffy, if we need one. Oregon and Japan are still embargoing us."

"Thank god you have some left," I say.

We sip our water of life. I ask: "How's your head, Kex?"

"I don't know. I'm worried."

"Let me take some readings."

- -

My wife is with me in the cafe, we sit on the patio. She sips her coffee and watches the sun set.

"How is your gut?"

"It's fine."

"You're still getting the upgrades?"

"Yes."

"I'm surprised they didn't cancel your insurance."

"Perhaps they didn't get around to it."

She is ferocious and quiet, plotting our doom, or our empire; both.

"You know I'm Chancellor now."

"A ridiculous title."

"Yes."

"Should I be proud of you?"

"No. Don't be proud of me. Wait to see what I do with this absurd authority."

She sips her coffee.

We move inside; it's getting cold. An antiseptic wash has been sprayed over the floors, affecting the taste of the coffee in my mouth.

One each table an ornate cactus is displayed, a careful transdimensional artwork, the fingers of the succulent interspersed with holographic projections of cacti from Chai-Murry.

I remember now why I became a professor, perhaps why most do; to stay young.

"What are you thinking about?" my wife asks.

"You. I'm thinking about you."

"Liar."

"I'm thinking about how beautiful you are."

She smiles, and I don't care then who I am, or what I have forgotten; she still needs me.

- -

Chai-Murry was Kex's idea. This fact is not a secret and yet it is not generally known. I believe that most have forgotten that Chai-Murry was Kex's idea not only because it is strange that a man's dream should have been translated into an actual dimension, accessible to all of us, but more because the maintenance of the Door requires our collective near-ignorance of its origins. Forgetfulness nourishes it.

But I am a cartographer. I am obligated to remember, and to chart these happenings into a form which my nation can use for our improvement.

I am back at the cafe, alone. The department chair has made arrangements for others to teach my classes this semester. The Chancellor's funeral is tomorrow. I am working on my elegy.

Have to send the old bugger off with the proper respect. He was a good man. Corpulent. Humorous. Highly sexed. Knew how to drink, how to entertain. A religious man. A family man.

In keeping with tradition his family has already been banished; their longboats like tears into the ocean only last night, to the mainland. I can remember the children's cries .
. .

For the first time I am grateful that I do not have children with my wife. I would not bring such suffering to them if I too fail; if I die at the hands of the Academy.

--

I am walking under the oaks, a lonely star in the chemical embrace of life, the caffeine warm in my belly and the chill air fragrant with the night. The small college town. The small college man. The light from the stars swirls over the trees and I find that I am here, really here, as though for the first time.

As though I just arrived.

Tell me, what is it? Do you know? What is that has come to us here? It is not Chai-Murry, nor Kex's idea that birthed its Door. It is something simpler and less knowable, something instinctive.

Is it evolution? Sadness? Both?

One of the oaks opens its door for me and I stoop to enter, scraping my back against the bark entrance, and huddling down, inhaling the heady acorn scent. The squirrel guard regards me from his perch within the trunk; his eyes see all.

Still I can smell their plot. The squirrels have been working on it for some time.

"What is it, squirrel? You're finally going to take over?"

It chitters at me.

I fall asleep, in the warmth of the oak.

--

Today I received a message, on my screen. The Emissary wishes to visit with me, before the funeral. I have already donned the customary funeral garb, my sleeves fitted with the velvety cardboard sheathes that simulate the branches of the oak; we are Druidical, we academics, we worship at the tree still.

With all the leaves around my face I can barely see, but it took me two hours to put this all on, so I can hardly take it off just for the Emissary. My wife helps me down the stairs; I'll have tea with him on the quad, where I have room to stretch my branches.

I kiss my wife's smooth elm cheek, tickling her skin with my leaves.

A wind comes in over the campus, smelling of sunflowers.

I fear I will have to leave. I will not be another sacrifice, if it comes to that. I will resign my commission and renounce my citizenship; I will emigrate.

But perhaps my plans will succeed. Slowly, so slowly, we leave the Middle Ages . . .

The Emissary comes with his hangers-on, literal hangers on, court dwarves arrayed upon his garments that trail behind him over the campus grass, clinging to the linen as though for their lives. He drags them over the soil.

I give him a small bow, as much as my tree costume permits, and smile through my leaves.

"Acorn?" I offer him my branch.

He smiles and takes one of them, crunching it between his teeth.

He speaks in Chai-Murrian and his chief minister, a willowy man with pale skin, translates:

"Thank you."

"Please sit."

I've ordered tea; it arrives in a steaming cauldron and I ladle out two cups for us; it is a bright and fragrant green.

He speaks, in his queer Frisian.

"Tell me that I do right, sir. My memory, it is fading. Are you well? You are well today?"

"I'm well, Emissary. I anticipate an era of strong cooperation."

"Yes. Yes. But others things too, eh? Something else . . ."

I sip my tea.

"I find I am grown lonely, Chancellor. Will you visit me in my apartments tonight?" His eyes are wide, slightly out of focus.

Why is the tower made from ivory? And why not soot?

"Yes, of course, Emissary. I will visit this evening."

His smile is dangerous; I find I cannot return it. I stand, and twist my arms, and shower his robes with acorns that his dwarves obligingly retrieve, stuffing the nuts into their pockets.

I make my way towards the cemetery, trusting to the Academy to guide me if I misstep; my field of vision is quite narrow through the leaves.

Chapter 11: The Funeral

I am a tree. I make the rustling sounds when asked; to guide
the Chancellor's spirit to the Great Grove in the Sky, or
wherever he may be headed.

Ancient shamans (a word from the Sanskrit, meaning
"laborer" — contacting the spirits is hard work!) traveled
great distances to share knowledge with other tribes. We
modern scholars are, in some respects, those old witch
doctors' wet dream: finally, time to study. The real work
can begin.

I stood erect and bristled my teeth, shaking my leaves, as
the earth was thrown into the grave, and when the pastor
had said his final words and the mourners remembered our
dear departed Chancellor, we processed from the grave, into
the quad, where we removed our clothes, and I removed
my bark and leaves, and we embraced one another.

Orgies are sad affairs, I often find, but they are necessary, as
they bind our fragile community together, and strengthen
marriages.

My wife has brought my tie and my suit. People are winding
down; few linger.

- -

I have never had a great fear of death; nor am I eager to visit
its kingdom. But I find that my work, cartography, is
actually related to our ancient burial-mound builders. In
them, you will find maps, of the dead. Whose spirit went
where, when. These maps are, in part, physical maps of
Earth, charting which burial-mound builders moved where
in Europe, back in the Stone Age, so they could remember
their cousins, and keep track.

Maps charted the astral wanderings of the shamans' souls. The aliens they met; the gods. The weird shit of all flavors.

Universities are not strangers to weird shit, in fact, we welcome it. The phrase itself, "weird shit," recalls the examination of excrement by shamans, to foretell the future.

All this is only to say that I am re-examining my scholarly identity. Am I only a colored-up shaman, full of mysticism and received wisdom, charts and maps of the spirit world? Does it matter?

It matters what you call something. Is the same action, named differently, a different action?

What are names?

Chapter 12: I am Chancellor

Things are back to normal now. We've left behind our medieval pomp, and can focus on our work. I have been neglecting my two graduate students and summon them to the quad. They are upset with me, understandably. Richard's beard is looking worse and worse; I like it. He's smiling, which could mean trouble. Cunegunde, or Koony, as we call her, doesn't look much better, though she's dressed very smartly. Her face is long.

"I'm sorry I've been out of touch," I say.

"We understand," says Koony. Richard nods.

"I've brought cookies," I say.

"None for me," says Richard.

"Please, take some."

"No."

"I'll have one," says Koony. She takes the lemon cookie delicately in her thin fingers, and begins to nibble around its edges.

"How is your research going?" I ask Richard.

"Good. We've isolated the event horizon on the Door; it appears to be a full inch out from the edge of it."

"Huh." I begin to nibble one of the lemon cookies too.

"Yes it took quite a bit of work to narrow it down, and it does fluctuate; we're monitoring it."

"Good, good." I consider a bit of bonhomie and a pat on Richard's back, then think better of it. He's a sensitive soul; he would sense my lack of commitment. "And Koony?"

"Roberto, I don't know what I'm doing anymore!" She begins to cry, and the sugar cookie falls from her hand onto the grass. One of the campus dogs bounds over immediately and begin to eat it. I pet it absently while holding onto Koony's shoulder.

"There there."

"You've been neglecting us, Professor," says Richard.

"I know and I'm sorry! You've seen how things have been! I'm sorry. Really."

"It's okay." Richard tugs shyly at his beard.

"I need a hug!" says Koony, and I give her one, and the dog rams its snout into my butt, smelling for all it's worth. I let it.

"How are things with your wife, Professor?" asks Richard.

I try to summon the right words, with Koony crying on my shoulder and the dog up my ass.

"We're fine. Just fine."

"I heard you're splitting up."

"We're spending some time apart."

"The reason I ask . . ."

I shoo the dog out of my butt. "Yes?"

"Well, Sasha asked me if I'd like to go to the Lawrence Livermore conference, and I . . ."

"Oh, go! Yes, of course!" I nod and smile, automatically. Yes, she will fuck this good-for-nothing graduate student. I can smell it. "Good for you!"

"I just wanted to make sure you wouldn't be offended . . ."

"No! No! No."

"Oh good. Well. My research partner is waiting. Don't worry about me Professor. Just keep signing the papers I send over, eh? Ha ha ha." He walks off, with his jaunty off-balance gait.

Koony's tears are beginning to dry up. The dog has bounded off after Richard, and I feel lonely. I look down at Koony's red face.

"Let's go get you some breakfast at the cafeteria, huh?"

She nods, looking up at me with her wide, mournful eyes.

Chapter 13

"Koony, when is the Lawrence Livermore conference?"

"Next week," she sniffs. "Are you going?"

"Me? Oh no. Too much to do here. With my new role. And everything."

"Professor. Roberto. You don't need to take me to breakfast. I . . ."

"No, I want to. I want to." I hold the door for her and let her in to the din of the cafeteria. We adopted the Japanese approach to communal dining here; faculty, trainees and staff all mixed together at the awful institutional linoleum tables. It's like being in the Army. We are soldiers of an obscure god . . .

I see Remy wave wildly at me; my first friend from when I first transferred here. I've been avoiding him; I feel bad. I wave wildly back, grinning.

I guide Koony towards the chef, whose mustache is very impressive, curled and everything; we're very proud of him.

"What will mademoiselle have today?" he says, his eyes French and romantic.

"She'll have the beef."

"I'm vegetarian, Professor!"

"She'll have the couscous."

"Oui," says the chef.

"And some green beans."

"I can order for myself!"

I smile and nod.

"And some Anatolian yoghurt please. In a yurt-glass," orders Koony.

Yurts come from Mongolia, not Turkey; but food never made any sense to me anyway.

I order the bangers and mash with the rocket garnish and guide Koony over to the table where Remy is grinning at me.

"Chancellor! Chancellor!" he shouts.

"Remy, please. You're embarrassing me."

He makes a great show of standing and then fawning, bowing like a peasant with great wide eyes, and the neighboring tables laugh.

"Your service pleases me, slave!" I shout at Remy, trying to continue the joke, but my timing has never been very good, and there is a silence then in the cafeteria. I help Koony get settled in, and then settle in beside her on the torturous narrow bench, waiting for the awful silence to pass.

"Chancellor, did you hear?"

"What, Remy?"

"The Ambassador, he vanished!"

"When was this?"

"Last night! In the middle the quad! Some of our Wiccans saw him! They were doing their moon dance, and they said they saw the Ambassador, by the fountain, you know the one I mean, the one where you bathe naked, Chancellor!"

"Yes . . ."

"He was washing his face, and looking up at the moon, and then *poof*, he was gone!"

"Incredible. How is the couscous, Koony?"

She nods, wolfing it down. She has a healthy appetite.

"The campus police were notified, but they could find nothing. Only his staff."

"His staff was left behind?"

"Yes, his scepter."

"Shit. Pardon my French. This is . . . bad, isn't it, Remy."

"Maybe it'll be good, Chancellor! Things are afoot! Ha ha ha."

"Yes. . . hmm. Koony, can I enlist your aid in a little snipe hunt this morning?"

"I'm always down for a snipe hunt, Professor."

- -

I am obligated, as an instructor at Eidon Academy, to continue to hold occasional office hours. But I also feel compelled to wear at least a sampling of my Chancellor regalia, to signify my new office. So I sit in the cubicle with the lowered ceiling with my miter on my head, and this obliges me to hunch a little, so that the miter will not damage the delicate ceiling, and so that the ceiling will not damage the delicate miter.

The fluorescent lights are beautiful.

Suddenly a student is here. I even remember his name; it's Mohammed – no, it's Badr.

"Badr!" I announce, unintentionally straightening my spine and crumpling the tip of my miter on the ceiling.

"Professor. I mean, Chancellor."

"Badr, good to see you. I missed you in class last week."

"I was experimenting. I want to go over the results with you, Prof."

Though there is some disagreement about its origins, I locate radiopathy's beginning with the performance work of John Cage; such as his Symphony for 12 Radios. Though at the time it was perceived only as exciting avante garde music, its healing properties became apparent several decades later.

"You had mentioned to me that Kex's face has been identified as a locus of dynamism vis a vis our region's developing phenomena," Badr says.

"Yes."

"I wonder, just what did you mean?"

"I don't know. It's the assumption I've been working with."

"But what could that mean, Professor? The lake swells don't seem to correspond with any of your data, for instance. And your radio shot into the mantle—"

"It didn't make it to the mantle."

"Close to the mantle, then, that shot only seemed to reinforce my own findings, that the lake is separate from the rest of these emergent phenomena."

"Perhaps it is. I don't know."

"But why would the lake be separate."

"Perhaps a Lady lives in there."

"Ha ha ha!"

"But seriously, Badr, you're doing good work. Would you step out with me to get some coffee? I'm beginning to find my office oppressive."

"Sure."

Badr is a good lad, excitable, in a good way. His beard is not regulation length, but we've softened those requirements in recent years.

- -

\- -

I'm looking at my wife's face in bed, terrifying.

Terrifying.

Terrifying.

How can I know her?

We look into each other's eyes.

\- -

Chapter 14: The Lawrence Livermore Conference

We are gathered here, dearly beloved, to bid goodbye to our linear accelerator. And our circular accelerator too.

I hold my wife's hand and Remy and Koony hold hands next to us, watching the billion dollar hardware spin out of California, into a dimension beyond our own.

Blue light spins out over the audience, seated on the warm brown hills of Livermore in late Spring, as the accelerators depart our world.

"It's beautiful, isn't it?" I ask Sasha.

She doesn't say anything; just watches. The blues spill over her face, and I kiss her cheek.

They're gone.

The sun is leaving too, and we lie back on our blankets and take out our wine and cheese and grapes, as the hundred other little groups do the same, enjoying the evening. Distantly, a modernist band strikes up their banjo/ synth-pipe-organ tune.

The world is ending.

Chapter 15: Kex

I am Kex. I am winding around a tree, that is you. Do not be startled, please, I am a tree too.

Qui êtes vous?

Ah, these lullabies are dangerous, for I am transmitting over a great distance and I can not be sure that it is received the way I want it to be.

Are you well?

Are you in my frequency?

It is not as I would like it; but, how I can fix that I do not know.

So it will be imperfect, which my friends here say is my nature anyway: imperfection.

My name is Kex but I have become part of what some call Chai-Murry. And some call it chimera. Some also call it Shim Shimmy Shim. I like to call it There-There.

Whatever you call this region, know that it is real, and that I am there, and also with you. I don't mean to sound religious; it is merely that I must try to describe truthfully how it is with me. I know it may be difficult to grasp all at once.

For one thing, I cannot, not exactly, say "I shall begin at the beginning" because the beginning does not exist here; it is so long lived compared to the universe wherein Earth makes her home that I might call here, the place I call "There-There," eternal, and it almost is. There-There is very long.

One thing I am quite certain of is that I am doing excavational work in the English language. Its idiom is heavily excavated in some areas; for instance, etymologically. The roots of English are quite well understood, back to the Proto-Indo-European. But its cognitive, or, if you prefer, spiritual, roots are not as well excavated.

So I am transmitting. My friend Roberto knows that I have the habit of changing many things when I act on Earth; that is because I am well-connected. Perhaps too well-connected. But not yet, I hope. I pray my distortion may still be adequate. Too clear a signal could upset everything.

I drip over wax. And I make a drum. I am luminous, and I am serene. I may even be a serenity, an idea of sereneness that shames the mere quality of being serene, in its horrendous depth, its longevity and magnitude.

Still, I must try to adapt to the idiom's needs. I must try to shrink, to adapt. I must try.

I am a visitor here, in Chai-Murry. In There-There.

It is a disturbing place to visit.

On Earth, many believe that space is three dimensional, and that one's eyes and ears and hands may delineate these three dimensions with very reasonable accuracy.

Of course, with the faintest consideration people have realized we are "prisoners" of our senses, and so with different senses we can perceive a different aspect of the reality we are enmeshed in. You do this every time you use a pair of binoculars, or drive in a car.

What I am is not a question I can answer confidently. In some centuries I would have confidently been called a monster, but that is irrelevant. I am not a monster. I am a man who has been some place else. A place I call There-There, for a very specific reason, and a place that The Chancellor calls Chai-Murry, because he does not want to believe that this place exists, even though he has already accepted The Diplomat and begun to make trading arrangements. I am more realist than he.

I see I have forgotten that The Chancellor is now Roberto. Still, like so many jobs, its institutional knowledge will begin to infiltrate his brain soon, and then I will have to contend with that. But that is why I chose Roberto for this task. He is my friend. He may yet come to know what it is that I have done, here in the There-There.

You remember how your mom would soothe you, saying "there there . . . there there."

I believe this region is soothing. That that is one of its chief purposes vis a vis its relation to Earth.

Chai-Murry is a place which soothes, even through dimensional gaps.

And this is dangerous, but also loving. It is mystical. It is something I have grown to know, and love.

Perhaps this means nothing to you at all. But I dare not broadcast for too long or this frequency may expand and occupy other bands which I know you need to remain open.

So goodbye for now. I wish you well; please believe that.

Chapter 16: The Lawrence Livermore Conference, continued

I listen to Kex's broadcast, with the rest of us here, wondering just what to make of it. He is a lunatic, I'm sure of it, but sometimes it seems to make so much sense . . .

The moon has risen; it is still warm. I look over and see my graduate students embracing, touching each other under the moon.

I feel suddenly shy, and sit next to my wife, electric, hairs on end, confused by I don't know what. Sex, I suppose. Even at my age I sometimes find it confusing.

I put my head on her shoulder, and close my eyes. I feel the wind. I hear the harmony of the Earth . . .

- -

I find I have slept. Most are gone but my wife has remained, loyal, my head in her lap, the moon gone. It is growing cold.

"You let me sleep," I say.

She gives me a strange look, and I sit up.

"Thank you for letting me sleep."

"It was nothing."

"We're almost the last ones here. The accelerators really went."

"Kex knows too much," Sasha says.

"Shh," I say, because I don't want to hear it.

"He's your friend. He's in danger."

She's probably right.

Chapter 17: Bomb Shelter

We're going to make winter.

I hadn't told you about this part.

I didn't want you to know.

My wife and I; well—

She said: "I need you. Come below."

And I did. To that place we said we'd never go.

The bomb shelter.

The California bomb shelter.

Certain acts invite certain events.

A map invites things, it cements avenues of thought, and one avenue I had grown fond of was change itself, but organisms can only take so much, only so much change. Yet homeostasis, in an environment, or a relationship, sometimes needs disasters. I suppose the question is: am I the disaster that was needed? Are Sasha and I still together, somewhere, beyond these dark lights?

- -

We're making winter.

We're making winter come.

This part I hadn't wanted to tell you. It is a surrealist part; perhaps it does not exist. Though it does. Still, perhaps it does not. We may comfort ourselves with that, if we wish. Perhaps it does not exist!

It is growing colder.

We hold each other in the cold.

It is very serious.

I hold my cheek against her cold brown hair.

She says, "Did you believe that I was your woman when we met, or only later?"

I say, "Ummm"

She says, "Did you believe that I was yours, and did that make you afraid?"

"Yes."

A wind is blowing. From Chai-Murry. Or just from the Arctic.

I can feel it through the metal walls.

Have you remembered yet why you sent us here? Into this continent.

Into this darkness.

I am a torch but I bear cold.

- -

I whisper in my wife's ear: "Will you love me forever?"

She says nothing.

I whisper in her ear: "I will love you forever!"

She says, "No."

A storm is blowing outside the shelter. One we have brought. We have turned off the radio; we're being very naughty. Who knows but that everything else has ceased to exist?

Except for the cold.

"I will hold your dust in my hands. When you are dead. I will celebrate your cerements with my nudity, and with my cock."

"Only if I die before you, jerk," she whispers back.

I laugh, and clutch her tighter, and outside the lightning starts, and the thunder.

Being the center is ultimately temporary but it is a quality California has grown used to, and we are rising to the natural height of our monument, a reasonable distance into the sky of the mind, marking our avenues and scraping our name out into the bones of the rock of us, the rock of us, the rock and roll of us, subsiding, slipping—

"No," she says, and holds me tighter. She's sweating.

It's getting even colder.

"When did we start?' I ask.

"Not long enough . . ." she says.

"What time did we come down here?" I ask.

"It will be enough . . ."

"What time is it now!"

"It's ten. Ten o clock." She's suddenly gone rigid.

The lights are out. I'm freezing; shivering, even in my robe.

I stand up and look at the dust that's washed over us.

"You did something very bad this time, Sasha," I say, and climb the ladder and open the hatch and look out at the quad—

(But that was some other me).

I don't want you to know about that part.

Let's just say (it's a cop out, Roberto, don't say it, don't say it—)

Yes, it's a lie, but I must tell it.

The bomb shelter was a dream. And I awake in bed.

My wife is gone.

The sunlight is the wrong color.

But everything else is fine.

I am still Chancellor. My miter rests upon my bedside table.

A low moan escapes my lips but my dog is here, my fond old hound. The dog I have named Doggus.

"Doggus!" He sits up, eyes bright.

"Bring me my computer!"

He fetches it from the living room, like a good boy.

I read the news. Trade negotiations with Portland. Japan is on strike. Arizona is talking nuclear disarmament. Governor Remington has done a photo op with his favorite shotgun, shooting skeet. The stock market . . .

There is no stock market, Roberto.

I know we have a lost a great deal.

And I believe that it in time, it can be recovered.

There is a danger in experiment, you see. The same as the danger of a trial.

No, not death. Death is not real danger, for yes, the experiment may well kill you, but even if it does the experiment will still have occurred.

No, the danger with experiment is this: having been done once, it can be done again . . .

Physics is as habitual as anything else, did you know? Like breaking in a new pair of shoes . . .

I must focus on my work.

Things get like this sometimes in California.

I put on the miter.

I take off the miter.

First I must shower.

Where is my wife?

Doggus is watching me. I scratch his head. I go into the shower. My lovingly well made shower; we re-tiled it only last year, beautiful Italian tile . . .

I shower. Longer than I should, but I do it, trying to shake the feeling that I'm dead, that I died . .

You remember, Roberto. California banned the stock market.

Yes, I remember now. Of course I do. We did ban it. For a while. My computer must not have gotten the upgrade . . .

No, that's not it either.

I must be losing my mind . . .

I shut off the hot water. I stand in the shower, naked. My body cooling. The water dripping down my chest, through the hairs on my belly, down my legs.

The dog barks outside the restroom. I wrap my towel around me and open the door, and the dog is barking.

The police are here.

"Hello, officers," I say.

"Mr. Oscuro?" They say.

"Yes, officers."

"Don't you have a doorbell in your bathroom?"

"I'm sorry, officers, no, I don't. What is this about?"

"Please, get dressed; we were worried about you. We'll wait in your living room."

"Please help yourself to coffee; or anything you'd like," I manage, stepping back into my bedroom. Doggus follows me happily.

How many things have I been forgetting?

No, I remember now. My wife. Sasha.

She wanted to play that goddamned game! She's going to get us in trouble. No, she already has. That crazy bitch.

I throw on white linen slacks, sandals, and a black T-shirt. I go back out into the living room.

The police seems so calm. I pause, like I'm lost in a dream. This dream that will not end . . .

I go to make the coffee. One of the officers is saying something. I can't understand him. I feel so tired . . .

"Officers, you'll have to forgive me, my work has been demanding a great deal of my time and I haven't recovered completely from the latest round of experiments . . ."

One of the officers, slightly skinnier than the other, with a small moustache, comes over to me opposite my kitchen counter. We have a full U-shaped counter; some people say it makes the food preparation area feel too presentational but I enjoy its theatrical quality.

"Are you okay?" the skinny cop asks.

"Yes. Thank you. Coffee?"

"No, thank you. Listen, your wife just called us over here because she was concerned. We've had a security breach on campus and protocol insists we keep an eye on all our top brass."

"Oh, I quite understand. What sort of security breach?"

"Someone came through the Door last night; no one was scheduled to arrive. The video cameras show someone emerging; then they blank out for several seconds. We couldn't see his face."

"It may be Kex," I say. The police raise their eyebrows.

"He was there, in Chai-Murry, visiting."

"Kex who?" says the second cop.

"My friend Kex. He lives here on campus."

"This friend of yours, he went through the Door?"

"Yes. He's a famous person, Kex is. But . . . you may not have been tuned to his signal. Forgive me. Would you like to see some of his videos?"

"This is probably going to be above our pay grade, but what the hell," says the skinny cop. "Show us the videos, sure. We can always forget we saw them later, ha ha ha."

I show them some footage of Kex; a short lecture, then just some home movies, him playing with his little yapper, him and an ex-girlfriend.

"He lives on campus?"

"In the penthouse."

"I guess that would explain why we've never seen him."

"You've never been up there?"

"Not allowed," says the bigger cop, who's standing, shifting his feet.

"Officers, I have a class to teach, and I wonder if it would be all right if I called you later?"

"Chancellor, of course. Just doing your wife a favor is all. It's nothing, really."

"Okay, well, thanks," I finish lamely, showing them to the door and trying to nod and smile.

I feel I've committed some crime. But I don't know what it could be. It was Sasha.

What did she do this time? Or what I have I done?

Chapter 19: The Badger

I'm banging on the old woman's door.

"Miss!" (What is her name!) "Miss! Please, I need your help!"

It's raining outside again. I had seen her with the badger, thrown over her shoulder. Its eyes mystical.

"Let me see the badger!" I shout.

She opens her door a crack; I can see her grey eye behind the security chain.

"Mr. Oscuro," she says.

"Miss, Madame. Please. That badger."

"What badger?"

"The one you were holding."

She shuts the door.

I bang on it.

My wife opens our door; her door now.

"What in the hell are you doing?" she says.

"Nothing, dear," I say, trying to convince myself hard of this, so that I might convince her. I stare at her.

"What do you want with our neighbor?"

"I had a question for her. It's very important."

"Well she never opens up for anyone. You know that. Come on inside; you're wet."

The old familiar retreat. The smells, and the useless throw cushions we chose so lovingly, beautiful and hard, unreceptive to human heads; handmade.

I sit on our couch; her couch. The rain is beautiful against the windows. I remember reading in history that Southern California used to be sunny all the time; it seems hard to believe now.

"She had a badger."

My wife sits down with our tea. So formal she is, at the strangest of times.

"Who had a badger?"

"Our neighbor! Your neighbor."

"I think she has a number of pets." My wife leans forward on the couch and touches my leg. "You look sick. Are you okay? Let me get you a towel."

She hands me one and I dry off my hair; I sip the tea.

"It's good."

She nods, watching me. I want to kiss her, but I know I shouldn't.

"I need to see that badger."

"Why?"

"The badger knows something."

"Oh, you've been talking to the animals again! What did I tell you about that!"

"I can't help it. If you don't believe, fine. I do. So do other people. They know a lot of things. Don't worry about it. It's not your problem. I should go."

"Don't go yet. Dry off first. The badger will still be there, I'm sure. I'm sorry. You can do what you want. You always have."

Chapter 20

I'm surfing.

Chapter 21

I'm reminded, suddenly, of the coup I performed that earned me my position here at the Academy.

Brian Bremlin, Associate Professor of Cartography, and my putative mentor when I first arrived in the department here at Eidon, had decided he didn't like me because we disagreed on the historiography of maps. Did maps represent memetic, emergent phenomena, or were they fundamentally human constructions with no will of their own? And so he had spread some vicious gossip that I was an abuser of horses, that is, that I had had carnal knowledge of a mare.

Like most departments in those days, we had a departmental mascot, which in our case was the mare Bessie, an even-tempered old thing, dull-white in color, fond of carrots and of shitting on the dean's lawn.

As you are no doubt aware, proving a negative is very difficult. How does one prove that one *has not had sex with that animal?*

I considered murder, of course, but in The Information State and our near-perpetual surveillance in all places and at all hours, murder is reserved for those high up enough to hire enough hackers to erase all digital evidence of the crime, and even then . . .

No, my coup was not a physical blow but an epistemological one.

I drew a map.

I drew a map of Bremlin's face, the first I'd ever done, the first face-map I'd ever drawn, and I drew it inaccurately.

I moved his nose far south so that is almost touched his mouth, and his ears I disarrayed so that they were not in agreement. I receded his hairline further and I made his eyes more even, the pores of his skin wider and more glaring, his complexion cloudier, his eyes' sclera more bloodshot.

It had its effects. The man suddenly had difficulty walking. He'd be climbing a staircase, and would suddenly stop, and stare, as though wondering just what stairs were, and what he was doing on them. Later he began to come to work only partially clothed, and not during designated orgy times.

My map was a powerful voodoo; something I had long suspected but never tested.

Bremlin was put on medical leave, and I took his job. As far as I know he is still in hospital; a medical curiosity.

It meant only a small bump in salary, but far more important was the status: I married my wife not long after.

His face, his real face, Bremlin's: I remember the look in his eye when I showed him my map. It was cruel, but he had done far crueler things. He had spoken ill of a horse. What kind of man does such a thing? A horse who had only ever served her community with dignity, and dropped large and generous turds on the lawn of the dean.

It felt good, of course, to have my just revenge, it felt wonderful, in fact, but it was troubling too.

He looked at me, and I knew then: I could become like him if I were not careful. If I abused the power I was now taking for myself.

And now I am reminded again of Bremlin's cold, hateful face, and that warning in his eyes.

I had hoped that in my new position I could "rule" by not ruling, I could govern by not governing, but I've seen that is not to be.

It is the homeless man. The one I fed not long ago, my leftover shrimp.

The homeless man has become the focal point of a vicious debate: what is to be done about him? Ought he to be housed? Should he be placed forcibly in an alcoholic treatment facility?

My position is that he is a free man and that he can lounge about doing nothing if he pleases, begging food and money as long as he likes, he has a nice personality, is not at all dangerous, but still . . . still—

Petitions have been circulating. Rumor spreads. And I have become the center of one of them: that the Administration of the Academy has resolved on a carrot-and-stick tactic, it is said, and that we are to declare to the poor homeless man: "go into treatment, or we will take away your food chits."

I am completely certain we are to do no such thing, I didn't even know the man got food chits, but regardless, the rumor spreads, and I am the center. It is said to be my idea, that I am a teetotaler (what a laugh!), that I hate the poor (I never thought much about them either way), that I am a crypto-fascist.

I see now the burden of this office: I become the shibboleth for all society's ills, I am the figurehead onto which all our sins may be transfigured, when the scapegoat is needed . . . I am him.

I ought to resign.

I have gone to visit Bessie, now in her dotage in the stable, Bessie of the big shits and sweet disposition; I have brought her some carrots. I stroke her nose and feed them to her, watching her kind, humorous eyes, wondering about the nature of power. The power of one mammal, over another. The power of one species, over another.

"Shall we give the homeless man an apartment?" I ask Bessie. She looks at me; it is like she is laughing.

Chapter 22

I realize, it's morning, I'm in my coed's bed, she's in class, and I'm in the student dormitory, a full professor at Eidon Academy, and I realize:

I must decide. What is it that I want? My life is passing its natural halfway point. What have I done? And what do I intend, still, to do?

I have no children. Do I want to have them? Do I want to have a baby with Michelle? Perhaps she's pregnant already . . . no, she's been careful.

Do I want to retain this ridiculous position of Chancellor? It is a ridiculous position. Almost completely meaningless.

My work: I enjoy my work. I feel I'm finally getting somewhere; understanding a part of reality I always wanted to understand, how things fit together.

Do I want therapy? No, not therapy. Too much like masturbation. I prefer fucking. I prefer action.

I must take us into the future.

I will retain my miter.

I will enter politics.

California: I love you.

Chapter 23

"Well honey," my wife is saying, "you're already *in* politics, hadn't you noticed? You're Chancellor! How much more 'political' do you want to get?"

"I have an obligation, Sasha, with what I know . . . an obligation to the state."

"Haven't I done enough for you! Did I ever complain? Did I divorce you?"

"Honey, you've been wonderful. You've been amazing."

"You're goddamned right. What office are you *seeking*, exactly?"

"A seat on the revolutionary committee."

She says nothing.

In the silence the clouds are moving over the sky. I look for my friend the crow but I don't see him; only some wrens, or sparrows, far away. Listening to their own politics.

"Why would you want that, Roberto?"

She puts her hand on my shoulder, and looks in my eyes.

"They could kill you," she says.

"No they won't."

"You don't know that!"

"I have faith."

"You're an idiot."

"I'm a believer."

"A moron believer."

"Will you support my running?"

- -

The neighborhood children are visiting today, like a flock of excited birds, swooping from tree to tree, with their minders hovering over them. A visit to university.

The mood of them, so bright and lonely, alive like I was once, storming the gates of reality, it is charming, but overwhelming, and I flee, into the higher levels of the library, so their voices are muted.

The women are playing lacrosse on the football field. One man among them, their coach, who is in red. The women are in white and black. I can see in their movements the burden of us, it is not like it was when I was a boy, even sport now has been affected by the burden of our new independence, we carry it warily, like a strange child or changeling, deposited on our shoulders.

I want to sleep but I can't. I take out my screen and look at the map.

One day some of the children will be trainees too. Sucked into our dark and livid maelstrom.

The map tells me nothing. I have my screen make a phone call, Elron, the chair of the Revolutionary Committee.

"Elron, how are you?"

"Roberto. Please. Call me Ron."

"The children are visiting today. They made me think of you."

"Ha ha ha. I am a child I suppose!"

"Well, I mean they made me think of the future. Of our state."

"Ahh."

- -

I've been put in charge of the espionage program. My cartography must go on hold for reasons of state. I haven't seen my coed for a month. She has a new boyfriend now. I remain sleeping on the couch.

I wake, and dress, and go out into the quad.

The sun is a brilliant blue, I squint watching the machines lay down the new cement; they are repaving the parking lot. Their cold red eyes regard me as they stamp down the shattered rock and oil. I know that it is racist, but I hate robots. And they hate us.

It hasn't rained since I last saw my coed. Two waters have been denied me.

I lay back in my medieval gown onto the brown grass, and I see the crow, four yards away.

"Crow," I say. And it squawks.

"What have you seen?" I watch its eyes, and follow its look, up at the sky.

My wife was pleased that I had been turned down, though she tried not to show it. She gave me a kiss, and then went to make one of her nude phone calls.

- -

I have decided to go through the Door.

The espionage program will have to go on without me; probably it will be better for it. And my real work can continue, on the other side of the barrier . . .

Book Two: Chai Murray

Chapter 24

It's light. Moving over me. I feel alive, but so confused. What was it that was taken? And what now is being given?

Tell me what you know. Can you? This ocean of stars and color, forming above me. It's like an avalanche, storming over me. I lie on nothing but I am contained. I watch. I wait. But what am I waiting for?

This life makes no sense at all. What is this life? And how does one make sense of it? And is making sense of life even the point?

I am a mast. But I am so small. And the wind is dark and alive. Vast. Vaster than anything I've ever seen. Aurora Borealis on crack. A kaleidoscope nightmare.

I am a professor but my profession is lost. What can I profess here? I speak openly, but ...

What do I say? And who is here to hear me?

"Hello ... ?"

Why did I never say anything to her?

To tell her how beautiful she was?

Does she know what this is like?

Like gravity. Come to rest. Paying a call.

Dipping its hat and saying:

"Hello there, good sir."

"Hello gravity."

"How are you today?"

"I'm ... fine, gravity. I'm fine."

I am a storm. I'm dipping in. I'm accelerating. Shooting through ... the door—

- -

Like that thing you see every day and never see. The question you never remember to ask. The hint, the hint—

Now I'm on the other side. I can see the priests waiting for me, for my cleansing. I'm sorry, honey. I'll be back.

Chapter 25: My New Home

The translation of my body to this plane I've found unpleasant; among other things, I can no longer hear my wife's voice in my head.

I am well and truly single.

I live now, much to my surprise, in a trailer park here in Chai-Murry. A well-appointed trailer park, one called "Highpoint Estates" and lauded as a "gated community," but a trailer park all the same.

My landlord, who kindly introduced himself to me again today, knowing that immigrants often have problems with memory, showed me a place where I could write, here behind the trailer, overlooking the arroyo. We've had some rain, and the water is flowing in it, though it is a dry country. Much like California.

Beside me are the landlord's plants, carefully labeled (in a language I cannot read), but with pictures I recognize: blueberries, blackberries, jalapenos, tomatoes.

The sun is different than I remember; redder. But the people are much the same, aside from the awkward fact that their English is so bad I can barely understand it. (Granted, my Chai-Murrian is non-existent).

The arroyo is quite beautiful, its stones like bones. The brown grasses like rotting flesh, pungent and rich.

Across the arroyo lies a mental institution; I can feel its sedative-radiation even from this distance.

Exercise is very popular about these parts, and one of the advantages of my view is the young women running on the path.

The old man, the landlord, sleeps outdoors most nights, under the stars on his patio, on a couch with a thin blanket; his bulk seems to keep him warm.

Translation is an ongoing problem, despite my implant.

Lying under the fading red light, watching the slow wind move through the arroyo, the landlord said:

"I moved here before they built the freeway. Before the war. All I have now is my daughter. She's smart as a whip; ask her anything, she'll tell you the answer. Or her computer will."

The daughter in question is very young, perhaps ten or so, but already quite beautiful, slim and olive-skinned with huge, devious eyes. I have already fallen in to the habit of obeying her, which I can see is an arrangement she is accustomed to.

I deeply regretted, at first, the lack of my screen here in Chai-Murry, but now I have come to see the advantages. Their technology may be backward here in Chai-Murry, but the habits of mind that this primitiveness brings about are invaluable, and have aided my own studies. Too, it has forced me to physically set down this narrative, something I might not otherwise have done.

When I return I can upload it; here, it is only ink on paper.

The priests here have offered me work, for which of course I am grateful. I've no desire to be homeless, here or in any dimension. I will teach English at the university.

Nassau County, the political district in which I've found myself, is a kind of aspiring-fascist city-state, and I, being of more democratic character, find I must hold my tongue when politics enters the conversation. Although newcomers are lauded here, and their opinions respected, I have seen too often how infatuation can pale quickly to dislike, if one reveals too much. So I decline English verbs by day, and by night, under the red sun's shadows here in Highpoint Estates trailer park, I go through one ballpoint pen after another.

- -

My first instinct was, of course, to write to my wife, but I quickly found that the bureaucracy I had grown so accustomed to threading back in California is even more Byzantine here.

I made several telephone calls but was only able to ascertain that messages passing back through the Door are "government business," which tells me almost nothing.

Today I have come to teach my first class and I regard my students, bright-eyed and deadly bored, innocent and jaded, young and old, gathered together to make new and foreign sounds in their mouth. I am their ticket to strange new worlds; to an escape from Nassau. Each of us imagines the Door leads to worlds of beauty denied us on our own side, forgetting that, whatever your travels, we cannot escape ourselves.

The ceiling fan soars above me in my rented room. I had worried a great deal, at first, about surviving here without Eidon's health insurance and my weekly upgrades, but the landlord assures me that a steady diet of beans will clear up any problems I might encounter; and who am I to argue with him? He does have a good recipe.

I eat the beans, with tortillas I've heated on the stove, and stare out into the parking lot, at the aging gasoline-powered vehicles, the heat-floating tarmac, and the grim-faced line for the washing machines.

I chew, and consider: why is it that I have come? What do I mean to accomplish?

Is it only another woman I want, only another mild adventure? Can I escape myself?

- -

Someone has been following me. I can smell it on my way home, on my bike. Not surprising, perhaps.

"Have you seen anyone strange come by the house?" I ask the landlord when I get home.

"Man, everyone around here is strange."

"Anyone you don't recognize?"

"You expecting someone?" His war veteran eyes regard me through a complex mask.

"What war were you in?" I ask him.

"Vietnam. When I was nineteen."

"How old are you now?"

"Sixty-nine."

"Just tell me if you see anyone, will you please?"

"Will do, boss."

He conveys his considerable gut out into the yard; he is building a new set of stairs.

- -

The animals here are different; they do not speak to me as they did at home in California. They are distant, aloof. One evening I watch a coyote watching me from across the arroyo, as though over an uncrossable gulf.

- -

I find I am forgetting things: the shape of my wife's face, the color of our California skies, the smell of the overcrowded cafeteria.

I have started drinking, something I never did before in earnest, but now I have a whiskey every night at six, something the landlord does not look pleased with, but he says nothing, and locks himself in his room.

What if it is Kex who is following me? Why doesn't he say hello? Is he someone different here on this side of the Door? Are all the maps of his face I've made, all I thought I knew of him, now null and void?

- -

I realize that I have gone mad. I came here and I do not even know why. The foreignness is oppressive; I must escape!

I climb out of the window of the trailer, into the trailer park, in the moonlight. I know the way to the Door. I must return to California! Before it is too late.

107

Chapter 26: Night

I am only a hologram now, on this side of the Door ; something wholly written. But still myself. The arroyo is moist; tentative and fragrant. This County is oppressive to me; even without its language it is oppressive. The spirit of California is not so here, despite their warmth, and their diligence.

It was good to visit; now I will return to honor my new crown, and my new city.

I will simply have to walk back through the Door; others have done it before me. Haven't they?

- -

Each house is nestled in its suburban kingdom, each apart and each alone. The silence is deafening, the quiet a music that is lonely and long and abiding . . . oppressive. I can see the glow of the door on the horizon, at the edge of their college.

Their college eschews its medieval roots here, unlike Eidon Academy it has no scaffolds or battlements, no gargoyles and wrought iron doors. Everything is clean and fine-lined. Business, of course, is what we have in common, trade, but it seems to mean different things on different sides of the barrier . . .

The door is unguarded. They've been moving it. Rolling it on its wheels to various points in the city.

Perhaps I will be permitted this small intrusion . . . certainly our California governors will understand my absence, a bit of frivolity, an honest excursion, my life hangs on the line but that's what life is, isn't it, a hanging . . .

The Door is in front of me. Gaping like a dark jewel. A liquid surface shimmers its hypnotic, rippling ink.

I watch the patterns form along its dark gilt edges.

I can see now that it is actually four doors, set inside the one larger one. But which of them leads to California?

One is red. One yellow and one blue. And one is a kind of grey. They all shimmer, the doorknobs changing, the wood paneling moving, but the colors are constant. Beckoning me to choose, like in a damned Shakespearean play, for the princess' hand.

It will be yellow. For the yellow California hills. I turn its handle and am drawn inside.

- -

And for an instant I see those fond hills but then it is something else. A nightmare yellow, waiting for me to eat me forever . . . I slam the door.

Now there are only three doors. The guard is come.

"Mr. Oscuro."

"Officer. Forgive me. I was on my way back to California."

He is so tall; his armor is dark, this guard. His voice is bass.

"You are entering a door."

"Ah, yes. Yes, I mean, with your permission, of course."

The guard says nothing but raises his armored arm towards the Door and the three smaller doors within it.

Red or blue or grey?

Not red surely. Grey then.

I open the door.

I can smell California, but then a great wind sucks the door out of my hand.

"You must pay a tax, traveler. You haven't paid," the Guard says.

"Ah, yes, of course. Let me see here. I have . . . fifty California doubloons, in silver! Will that do you?"

The Guard takes the money in his metal hand and looks at it a moment before dropping it into his pouch.

"No," he says.

"Ah. How inconvenient." I make a grab then for the grey door's handle then but the Guard stays my hand.

"Pay," he says.

"My wife can pay you," I find myself saying. "As soon as I return she'll have a bank draft ready, of course. Six hundred doubloons. More than generous!"

"Six hundred?"

"Seven! I'll bring it to you tonight!"

"Yes. Bring it to me. But you are not going through until then."

I leave the Guard to his Door.

\- -

Kex is waiting for me at my neighborhood's only bar. The only patron at this late hour. As though we met here in this strange dimension every night.

I put my hand on his shoulder.

"It's good to see you," I say.

"What will you have?"

"Whiskey."

Kex watches me while I watch the bartender pour; suddenly I am famished for the alcohol and I drink half of it at once.

"You needed that."

I nod. "Thank you."

"How long have you been in Chai-Murry?" he asks.

"A few weeks."

"Roberto. Why did you come?"

"I need money, Kex. I need to go back."

"You can't go back."

"What do you mean?"

"Even if you go back, you won't be back."

"This is some philosophical bullshit you're selling now? You never used to be that way, Kex. How are you feeling?"

Kex looks away and brushes his hair with his hand. "Fine. I'm fine, Roberto. But listen. You're not going back. Not the way you think, anyway."

- -

Something has gone wrong. I can feel it. Not just with my wife, with everyone. I can almost feel the crow's eyes, accusing me, as though saying, *you should have known this earlier.*

- -

"How then?" I ask Kex.

"Through me."

"You mean we're going to have some kind of creepy interdimensional sex? I love you, Kex, but I'm not ready for that step in our relationship."

"No. I love you too but it's not that. I'm going to have to play shaman."

- -

Shaman means *worker* in Sanskrit. Religious magic is hard fucking work; same as a scientific revolution, don't I know it.

Shaman dancing is galactic tragedy, is religious energy, it's traffic on the bridge of universes, simple shifts of balance on the soul, the ritual august and true a laugh and a shrew, stewing over your obtuse remove from everything you knew, but didn't want to—

Kex grasps my hand.

"Are you ready?" he says.

"Fuck me."

Theocracy and autocracy remember the shaman, but it depends on the man: as everything does, it depends on you. Governments, and dimensional gateways, are only as strong as the people who comprise them.

- -

It's the power of prayer we need, and this makes me uncomfortable as I'm still technically an agnostic liberal academic, but I'm also a scientist, and I go with what works.

We work the phones like lovers, talking into the ears of Nassau County, but the problem is, the problem is, they believe in Jesus here in Nassau, and news of a little religious wonder coming home to roost amidst their comfortable suburban ruin will not exactly be welcome. We gotta move fast.

"Hello ma'am do you believe in the power of prayer?"

I'm working my way through the phone book.

"Umm. Well, yes."

"Will you come to a prayer meeting to save a soul this Saturday?"

Kex says we need one hundred believing bodies, to send me through, in a gateway of his own.

I can feel the crow's mind, somewhere near to mine, hovering and watching, laughing—

- -

The men and women, true believers in the power of prayer, god bless their innocent hearts, are moving over the grass of Hart Park, towards our prayer circle.

In the Jewish Kabbalah, God is described as having many faces, many of them accessible only to the initiate. I map faces; but in their mapping one reveals the fluid dynamics of expression and personality, the uneasy gaps between what is and what we might believe to be, ordering the cosmos and exacting our prize, or curse, or sentence, in our effort to understand. In hart Park over the grass our brave followers, temporary sitters-in to prayer, their faces come under the light of this foreign sun. They're just like me, wondrous and serene and wonderful, God quotidian unknowable but still being mapped, by all our eyes—

We join hands.

- -

Judgment is a separation; this is why the judge in the fable is prefigured on the pot (shit also comes from a root "to separate"). But a Door is a joining, and so this prayer circle is a strange amalgam of separation and joining, judgment and forgiveness—

I am to remember. I must.

Here is how it happened:

Chapter 27: Sasha

Her name originates in Central and Eastern Europe where it was originally a diminutive of Alexandra, and so can be said to mean "little defender of men."

Like a shepherdess. Like a holy stone.

I imagine her nude, now, standing like a dolmen, awash in rainwater, her breasts arced towards the road leading up into our camp at California—

I met her only after I had come to Eidon. She was three years older than myself; thirty-six.

We married within a year of meeting.

The hypnosis of woman is like the hypnosis of memory; it is a thing of smell.

She smelled good, of course, spicy and electric, solemn, enebriatic, fortunate, edged with grief and hope, alive, so alive I knew she was, more even than me, who count myself fortunate to be a passionate man.

"What do you want to do to me?" she had asked, and I told her.

- -

Why did I allow myself to ignore so much? My wife's investments. The coming of the Procuratorship; the Protectorate of California as the island floated inexorably north, towards Alaska, following tectonic urges, tying its financial destiny ever tighter to the bettors on Wall Street with every passing hour—

I wanted her body but I ignored so much else.

- -

California is a city-state; as you know. But now I must tell you of our destiny; what we paid for our happiness. And what we used our happiness to buy.

Crow

I am the crow.

--

I derive messages from out of the ether.

--

Tell me, what will it be when we arrive?

Are we to remember anything?

Are we to know what to do, then?

Having arrived, having remembered, is it enough?

Something has happened. I am remembering. Everything I knew is gone--

Some terrible doubling--

God, help me

Chapter o

"You see this region here?" I pointed at Kex's left eye.

"Everything he sees, and everything we see in him, is contained within his eye. But in mapping an eye, we are mapping consciousness, and so then the question becomes:

"What do we want to be capable of thinking?

"What do we want our being to consist of?

"It is a decision, simply put, and not idly undertaken, a decision that will change everything that we are, and may become."

Chapter: -1

I am in California, but something is not right. My wife is with me. My former wife. My current wife. Sasha.

"Sasha, what is it?" I ask her.

"Shhh," she says.

The arm is crawling across the lobby, like a metal snake, bound for my gut; it attaches to my belly and begins to do its work. I lie back in my chair. The trainees gossip. The televisions are a drone. My wife is disrobing in the phone booth.

I am floating, over the city . . .

I am a crow.

I'm a professor.

I'm a cartographer.

The map inside my mind is fitful, untrue, retarded. Growing. New, soiled and wet, lively. I can feel it quivering, underneath my forehead.

I will map, but what then? When we have all seen what I do?

I follow the homeless man away, he is crunching on the shrimp.

I have disconnected from my upgrade prematurely . . . the metal arm is trailing from my gut, like a thoughtlessly discarded petrol nozzle.

The homeless man turns his head and looks at me with his eyes, warning. I follow him into the alley and he opens a door.

- -

"Roberto, we've missed you! So much!"

She is in my arms.

The music, where does it come from? I am dancing. The only thing I was ever meant to do. Kex, is he human? Am I?

Something has gone wrong. I can feel it, in my gut. In my head.

I am dancing. The candlelight is beautiful and I lie back on her broad bosom and hear her whisper in my ear:

"Roberto, we've been waiting for you. Are you okay?"

I manage a nod.

"Listen, I brought something for you." And she holds a small cake underneath my nose and I open my mouth, and she places it on my tongue . . .

Chapter: -2

I am making love to Sasha. In our bedroom. The ceiling fan spins overhead, over her head, as she climbs atop me.

Her body is melancholy. The room fills me with something—is it like when I fill her? The room fills me with expectation. And with fear, a warm fear like summer coming when I was a boy, the eternity of those three months, the heat, and the fear, spreading over my body like a thick paste—

She is panting. I am smiling. But what did I decide?

Is this what I decided on?

When did I make the decision?

Did I really make a decision?

Jetzt oder nicht, naturlich, aber — but . . . I can remember something.

Pushing into my mind like I push into Sasha, clasping her ass in my arms. The map.

The map.

Kex is like a map container. Like a starmap. He has been encoded. Why isn't a question I can answer, but the how: he is the reason for the Door. He is the focus of my misadventures, of all of ours. A kind of reverse avatar, once one of us, he has now ascended, not cognoscenti but guinea pig . . .

I must help Kex understand what I am, who I am, or rather: I must help him help me understand who I am now; who I have become.

My miter is not arbitrary. My head is not too heavy. I am chosen, or have chosen myself, but my purpose—I must undergo it all again, first. First, back through these gates, and then, then I will be able to remember—

Sasha is angry with me; I shut off my mind and concentrate on her.

Chapter: -3

It's raining again. Part of me remembers being here; I brush it away. I fidget idly, poking at my screen, making random patterns in the red ribosomes mapping the rainfall at the fountain; the coed is there.

She is there, her eyes like stars, I open my mouth:

"Not you," I say.

"Excuse me?" she says.

"Oh, excuse me. I mean, help."

"Are you okay?" She comes over to me. I drop my screen into the puddle of water; it fizzles out.

"You ruined your screen," she says, looking down. Water floats in her hair, her eyelashes.

"Kiss me," I say.

She laughs. "Are you drunk?"

"I wish I was. Take me upstairs, please, I need to be indoors."

"You're Professor Oscuro."

"Yes."

I hold her hand and she lets me. We step inside the dorm. The guard regards me with suspicion.

"He's ill," she says. "He needs help."

"Should I call the paramedics?" the guard asks.

"No, I'm just going to make him some tea."

This repetition, it is like a rehearsal, but for a show which is steadily worsening, its drama thickening, its tension lengthening, its escape nigh impossible—

We have reached her room.

"There are holograms in your room aren't there," I say.

She looks at me. "How did you know that?"

"I've been here before," I say.

"You're freaking me out," she says.

"Sorry. Here, I'll sit. Please, tea would be wonderful."

I slide down the wall like a drunk, down to my haunches, lost in my heavy awareness of all that is happening, all that is still to happen . . .

Some of the other coeds walk by me, watching me, I try to smile and don't quite succeed.

The hallway is oppressive but at least it is quiet. So well behaved, these young women. Like princesses, girding their loins with the law books of worlds yet to be.

She emerges with my tea; it smells delicious. She sits beside, puts her arm over my shoulders. Looks at my face. I do not flinch from her gaze, though I want to; I am so weak.

"What are you doing here?" she asks, fingering my beard.

I sip.

"Hmmm."

"Such a strange man."

"Mmm."

"Are you married? Oh, you are, I've seen your wife."

"Yes."

"Are you happy?"

"I've gone insane."

"Oh honey, we're all insane here," she says.

Chapter: -4

Why did I become who I am now? Did I choose it, was I forced into it? Both, I suppose. Why can't I remember? I don't believe the truism that it is the nature of memory to be obscure, to be inaccessible. Something has happened. Someone is keeping me from what I need to know.

The Ambassador arrives next week. But he has already arrived. No he has not arrived yet.

How does one make peace with insanity? And if everyone shares your hallucination . . . what is the problem? The problem is: I don't like this hallucination. Even if everyone else does. I want to be normal again.

Make me normal, God. Make me normal. Make me an upright member of society. Make me unafraid, and unapologetic. Make me mercurial without doubts, and steadfast with no regrets. Make me a rock. Make me a stone. Make me the giant shoulders for the generations of the future, make me Gibraltar, unredeemable irrecoverable unstoppable dynamite in every cell of my body . . .

I am in the shower. I have been crying. I shut the water off. The noise in my throat is like locusts.

"Honey?" My wife is outside the door.

"I'm okay," I say.

I hear the door shut; she has gone out.

I am alone in the apartment. I am supposed to be at the Ambassador's reception; that must be where she has gone.

I am to take a photograph . . . no, Kex hasn't given me that order yet. The photograph. Was that all that was wrong? I took the photograph, and then . . .

But maybe it happened before the photograph.

Maybe it happened when California broke off from the mainland; when it began to float free, like one of Juno's isles, blessed and hermetically sealed from all evils, a Mediterranean Eden . . .

I dress and go outside. The crows avoid me; they fly away when I look at them. The old woman with the badger is nowhere to be seen. I follow the stragglers towards The Great Event.

Chapter -5: The Photograph

I have the camera in my hands. I know now what we have done: we have seceded. Not just from the Union but from the consensual reality we shared in that union.

Why is the photograph forbidden? I cannot remember. But it is.

I raise it to my face and aim at the Emissary through the eyepiece.

- -

When I was a boy I loved cameras. It's probably what led me to mapmaking, because what fascinates me in both is composition; where one draws lines.

What is the relationship between a set of objects and people and what are their borders? The mapmakers and photographers decide. They show us how to see.

But there are so many ways to point the camera.

- -

I see his face, the Emissary's, his huge nose, swollen and red, almost a lymphatic cancer, an enormous nose, and his strange eyes that seem to rest somewhere other than his head, even though they're right where they're supposed to be, above his nose on either side of it.

I press my finger on the button to expose the filament to the light.

There are no words for what happened next; or perhaps it's fair to say the majority of the words I have so far expended in this telling are for what happened next, this nauseating doubling, and my terrible ennui, ennui that is no longer a mere French boredom or malaise but a suicidal weight of madness, insisting *everything makes sense* and that nothing ever did or will ever make any kind of sense, nor can it ever do so.

The world was black and I was a speck, torn in its blackness like a wave, like an intruder, caught in a house without borders or windows, doors or roofs, only walls without end, stretching forever I press my palms against them, under the foundering daylight as the guards crush in around me and they shatter my camera on the flagstones.

There is no color but there was never any color, and time is a nightmare but it is a recurring one, with specific images that show up again and again, the images:

A cracked window.

A river of glass.

A baseball.

A boy and his bat.

The field, grey-green, stretched in the distance where he stands, holding the bat idly, watching the clouds, and the reaction of the wronged parties one hundred yards away.

My hand, told so many times, by so many, told who it is, it recalls, more than muscle memory, my hand is the image of time too, curved and tired and unafraid.

Sasha. Her lips. And her eyes. Her waist.

I accept the handcuffs and I move through the crowd, transgressor, the guards pushing me forward. Kex will pay.

BOOK THREE

What can I remember now, I who came underneath the gun? I sit and I remember, but memory is like experience, it comes over me, and I think:

Which one is real? And how did I become this way?

Was it only the drug?

Was it only the experience of the drug?

Or was the drug designed to trigger exactly this, and if that trigger is real, what does it mean?

Only an accident, like the Big Bang?

- -

I hold her hand in the lobby and she speaks to me, but I am listening to the *otherwhere*, the place that I have been. The place that I am going to again.

Outside is the cage where the smokers linger, looking down on the freeway.

My shirt has begun to stink. I haven't washed it; I haven't had the energy.

In front of me in line the old woman opines: "Whew! Somebody stinks today!"

She looks at me, and says: "It's you, isn't it? That shirt will stand up on its own!"

I smile and agree.

I go outside with the crowd, watched by our overseers, and the girl who holds my hand will not come out; the smoke bothers her.

Below, the freeway is like a small god, urgently speaking to us of what we have lost, of what we will continue to lose.

I remember now: I am in the hospital. For what I did.

- -

I tried to repeat too much, too excited by my new theories, too avuncular when it came to their experimentation, too willing to risk myself, like so many scientists before me, in the proving of it.

I am the proof but the proof is hidden, inside the hospital; perhaps it is designed that way. Get too close, these days, and we have ways of making you talk, Lebowski.

I hold her hand and I remember. The coed whose name I keep forgetting. And the face of the crow like the face of time, curved and cruel, waiting, waiting for someone to speak its name true into the air to shaft the light in that particular way, in that particular way when I am come to speak, come to work my magic, come to start the chain reaction—

We dine in the room.

We receive our pie.

The President is speaking; he has grown a beard. I sit to his left. He is speaking on the phone inside his head.

"I've been captured!" he says. "You got to get me out. Is my limo ready?"

We are sardines awaiting processing; or this is the processing.

Obey and you will be saved; we are Christians in this way, the obedient are saved. And the disobedient . . . they are tested.

- -

They let us outside today. The soda machine was like a small and terrible god, lined up and supercooled, we wait in line, to buy the Cheetos and the Dr. Pepper, every nickel is a fortune inside, cheap cigarettes the new Jerusalem, I am a shadow but I'm growing.

Is this my penance, my absolution, my salvation, my ticket to ride—

- -

"Tell us about your experience again, Roberto."

He sits back in his chair and crosses his arms, carefully, secure in his knowledge that he is a small and heady genius, like Napoleon, only crueler and with fewer armies to do his bidding. He has drugs for that.

"I hate you so much. I hate you with a purity I thought impossible, for I abhor purity, it is so dangerous, like Purity of Essence, that terrible mad captain in The Big Lebowski, I mean in How I Learned to Stop Worrying and Love the Bomb, Dr. Strangelove, purity is too religious, too hierarchical, too much a machination of the temple, but it is so with me now, this purity of my hate for you. Not too pure to work but pure enough to linger, to grow and change, like a cancer, like a new organ, like a relationship.

"I have a relationship with my hatred of you," I continue, as he watches through cruel, amused eyes, "like a relationship with a former lover, eyeing her uncertainly, wondering what is to come now, what is this afterwards. But the after is before, I am hesitating before the jump, of what my hatred will mean."

"This hatred you're talking about, Roberto, it's only hatred of yourself—"

"No. It's *you* I hate. It's you. You don't want to know that but I'm telling you. And you've earned so much hate. So much."

- -

Does it matter if I don't know what time or city or year I'm in as long as I know myself?

At last.

At last this time comes when I know myself, not in a fever or in a dream but while I am awake, like knowing the Mississippi, on which you must mark twain because it always changes, because the Mississippi cannot be predicted and cannot be mapped, because the face of the river is like the face of God, hovering over you a transmission frequency, obedient to every utterance of the waves, every undulation of the current, transmuted holy into our eager hands, the water:

I am in California.

But which one?

Out of the Hospital

The Academy is in me like the memory of a drug, like alcohol for the one who's just climbed on the wagon, a shadow so palpable it's more real than the guy next to you.

I move in the car of my roommate over the Los Angeles highway.

I fear I have gone so far ahead there can be no tracing of my route, should I ever wish to return—

What of my wife?

I feel her close.

I feel her so close.

The crow hovers over our car, stopped in traffic on the interstate.

- -

I know I am being punished. But what was my transgression?

Only the marijuana? Ridiculous. My May December dalliances?

No, it was something more . . .

"Tell me again. Tell me again, goddamn it, I need to remember!"

Sasha's like a ghost now, walking beside me, this bitter hologram, but still loving, despite, despite my betrayal, and my abandonment—

"You were something they needed, Roberto. They made you, the Academy. You're still their tool, even now," Sasha says, flickering.

"No I'm not."

The Los Angeles sunlight is more powerful than any drug imaginable. And the people at the bus stop are used to people talking to themselves.

INTRALUDE

A Lullaby

For if I shall come to you a lonely one, a light over a wave,
it is not intransigent to insist that it be now, and that it be
now, to hold that

triangle at the sky, in your hand--

Let it be now avast ye for this simple game you're folding in
your hand, it's so large you may not see it all at first,
but wait,
just wait,

A part will be revealed--

But if I reveal that, if I reveal that, then you must reveal
something too.

Is it any wonder that you were ready to come, when I was?
(In that clearing).

Expostulation or demoulement, untoward but true this
lightning echo of the you you were, before I knew you--

- -

The Garden is a city of the mind and I outdrew you there
but not yet, not yet --

- -

A thousand intersections. And a chance gesture. A heated argument and a time in that city that we spent before we moved, in New York--

I felt I knew you then too.

And I did, but I have to forget now, I have to forget now to make it truer than it was, to make a claim on your verdict of my identity, my

sameness and difference come at last to a decision--

The me you'll need, or remember that you need, after I am gone--

- -

Like a flycatcher or a hope written onto paper, the game of house and the fate of children wrapped inside its folded carriage, one tow three four one two three four,

We rehearse the dogs of war bark bark with every liberated page,

Torn out to rest between our legs, this verse of fire, my body your tool, this , this, sentence a recapitulation of your movement and my

insistence, your cold and my heat on top of the sheets, of grass--

- -

It is soon and I am afraid.

- -

Over the seasons she came in and I watched remembering
that *that* her was not the one that I remembered, and --

"What are you going to do?"

"What?"

"You look dangerous"

"I am dangerous"

All without words, or without those words, of course, this
is only a memory, but a precise one--

- -

I am remembering. It is not right, but there it is. As of a
verse, caught between endings:

I am righteousness. That is, I am this thing that must be, and
is, for a moment--

Like in an argument. A folding in, and down, to the beating
heart of what I know we need--

But you disagree.

You say it's a common thing, disgrace, and that we can have
no better,

For are trodden things, worn and wasted and gone--

It's okay to remember, I say, it's okay--

There is no night in the forest,

There is no night in this forest,

Not with me,

If you'll believe,

Not in something disastrous,

Or ridiculous,

But simply in the logic of the argument, of things coming to bear,

And certain resemblances,

AS between light and your eyes,

Or the music and a bough,

Of a tree.

--

Come unearth to me,

I am waiting,

On your bow my banner or a dream,

But that's too much.

- -

Counting seconds is wrong

Like counting trees

Even the mood is not quite it,

It's the reality of it

That is what I'm after,

What is the reality of it?

This reality of it,

This reality of it.

My words and your voice,

Not the same,

But similar,

Disjunct adjunct frequencies at voice to trembling and embrace with heat and violence the shape of the face of that terrible cleaning, that garden and city,

My love a force of cold and breaking poison exquisite and fated for knives and excellences untranslatable into the language you have

brought and so let me rearrange your tongue, and let me reassign your movements on this abattoir of thought, the dance,

The dance is abattoir of thought al hanging with t heir sentences and shapes now for us opt take and drape over your minds--

Drape me, Sasha,. Drape in this meat world, drape me in this meat world for I am a canyon and I am a thought,

I am your canyon and I am your thought,

Made with this exacting need--

- -

"it's not what I was thinking" you said

And I said, "Yes"

And you said, "Why?"

And I said, "I don't know"

And you said, "Ha ha ha ha ha"

And I said, -----------------

- -

It's not over because I remember your face,
I remember it with me,
Though it was not, not with me, not exactly,
But close enough--

- -

One two three.

I'm yours.

What do you want.

You want to know how it was.

You want to know what it meant.

You want to know why I'm carrying on like this.

Well you can carry on however you like.

With or without me.

- -

Which is it that you want?

I have to give you the hard version, because the easy version won't explain anything, and at its most simplified it is not different from an equation:

$1 = 0$, or "time and space sure do exist!"

These simplifications are not useful. I must explain, and explaining does not simplify; it complicates.

Now that we have that out of the way we can proceed with my simple story, of me and Sasha, and the way the world ended,

And the way I brought our Jerusalem into the world, not because it was easy, but because it was hard, and it's only a walled city on a after all, only a mind, with a fancy name for a God, some God mostly forgotten now but defensible, like a strong mind.

A defensible mind, yes, but a defensible mind must have exists, Sartre was wrong, because hell comes in so many shapes and sizes, so many shapes and sizes you can hardly imagine.

And so I must define for you *this* hell, the way it was, not then and not when you are reading this, but now.

And now.

And now.

Und jetzt.

Und jetzt.

Und jetzt.

Und jetzt.

Yes my body and yes your body and yes that desert and yes those trees and yes this revolution, but not a violent one, that is, not with guns, but with words, more violent than any conflict in the battlefield, words are the most hideous weapons ever devised by man, and used by women and men, and then by children, hulking over this old ground, forever-

Forever and forever and forever and forever-

For always in the soul I'm with you though you're dying.

Though I'm dying.

But this soul is a bodily thing and I must explain how it came to be,

How I came to be this soul that you see before you now,

How I came to be this soul that you see before you now, this body and this work,

My love it is only getting closer but it is already now,

It is already *jetzt* and it is already now in that garden of our soul together, Sasha,

I am dying now.

I am dying now.

I am dying now and you remember.

You remember because it was how it had to be it had to be that way and –

I must tell you everything.

- -

In San Francisco I was a boy and I grew up a noble savage of a man. I grew up a noble savage of a man and that's because San Francisco means Saint Freeman and so do all the people of and the tribes of the world often translate to either "People" or to "free men"

Because that is who we are these prisoners of freedom and I bought something.

A ticket south.

Into slave country.

Los Angeles./

Los Angeles slave county I am come and though I shall forget I remember too, in terrible Romanticized fashion, the logic of your coming true—

Have you ever been to Los Angeles, Sasha?

- -

Be Mimetic, Roberto, Be Mimetic, and paint as with a
sword over the body of the brain, perform this surgery that
we must all awrit---

- -

Be descriptive.

Be prescriptive.

Be proscriptive.

Be ingenious. Disingenuous. Noble and afraid.

Be everything you can be. AN army of one. With four
quarks inside, up down charm and strange, O up down
charm and strange hold me tighter than a hurly burly, hold
me tighter than a cumming Ophelia, hold me tighter than
the Damascus steel over your beating heart, baby—

Can you remember—

TELL ME THAT YOU CAN REMEMBER

Sasha

My name is Sasha and I am a woman.

I first met Roberto when he was in college, in Jerusalem.

We speak English but we speak Hebrew too, and my name is a Russian name, because my grandparents were Russian, fleeing the pogrom, and Russia means "row" because it was founded by Vikings.

So I am a Viking Jew, and a Russian Israeli.

And an American.

I am forty-five years old.

I resemble my grandmother, a madwoman. Though not in appearance.

And though I am afraid, I am sterile.

And though I am dead, I am alive!

And Roberto made me feel alive, on my last day in Jerusalem, when I thought that I would die, but I didn't, and he didn't, and then we made love, and I came to cartography as to a lesson I'd been wanting, a lesson I'd been wanting so hard I could barely believe it, because when he came I knew I'd found someone I could love, but more than that, I'd found someone I could use, and I used him so hard I could barely believe it, and he let me keep on using him, harder than anything I could believe possible, and that is how we came to the Academy, and how my rebirth as a scholar of these strange lights of ours came to be.

What is it to be a Californian?

It is to be a prisoner of the imagination.

For though York exists (originally *Eborakon*, meaning "yew tree estate"), and so we have New York, as its memory, California exists only in the dream of that Spanish novelist, and the sailors who dreamt with him, of the magical things that they would find in Baja (mistaking Baja for an island, those first Spanish sailors named California for a imaginary and magical island in a famous Spanish romance novel published in the early 1500s), beautiful maidens, and green green grass, and the red red blood and all the beauties and terrors of the New World, unimaginable, which were the inheritance of our forefathers, those mad Spaniards, and the logical evolution of this obsession with imagination ,a healthy one, I believe, but an obsession nevertheless, is something very close to solipsism, but not quite solipsism (which is the notion that your mind is the only mind, and no one else exists, and so a very evil delusion), but this close cousin of solipsism is simple Jerusalem, a stubborn motherfucker, and the Jews are known for many things, and known accurately and gratefully and obtusely and horrendously and spiritually and all those ly-s for being stubborn, for Jews are not solipsists but they believe in Jerusalem, as we all do, because it is a tough nut to crack.

I have been broken over the storm of California, and in my healing I am yours, for a time, your storyteller, and Roberto tells me that this narrative is being transmitted to you live, and I am grateful for that, I believe it gives me a certain freedom in our time together, for I know that surely I spell not only my own death sentence and perhaps Roberto's as I tell this story, but likely the death sentence of our little Jerusalem, the city I helped build here in California.

151

My California is not the California you remember, and it is not the California I first saw when I came, but it is a California I have made, almost all on my own, and in this I am a true Californian, for we all come here to realize the truth that the truth is of our making, and we make it so differently, like Irishmen, true for you, hey, true for you, and it was true for me, young and in love with Roberto, an then with California.

And though we will have no children I can believe that the children I will have are you. That you are my adopted children for this narrative, almost beyond my won belief, will be the change of all of you. And is that really so remarkable? IS that not all language is? A mind control device from beyond the moon, a terrible gift and birthright, like being Jewish, that you can not escape when the Russians come, and so you must own it, you must own the murder of our tongues and what we have come to do with them.

Well here is what I have come to do with mine, I've come to do you, honeychile.

And so let me tell you the story of Roberto in California and the life we built together and the life I helped murder, for though I am a Judas in this story, it may be that I am the secret Judas that the Gnostics wrote of, who shows you the secret door out of this universe---

- -

Even Roberto's typographical habits are rubbing off on me; I've watched him write so much.

Tell me, what is cheating?

Is it a cheat to be a human being?

Is it a cheat to be made of this flesh?

Is cheating lying?

Is the universe a lie? That is what the Gnostics believed but I don't believe that, only that the universe is a truth too complicated for us to understand, and we have an obligation to make peace with the partial truths we have come into possession of, adapting and reversing and evolving them, each to our own but shared to, an argument that is life.

I cheated but I did it cruelly, knowing I made use of my body as I had made use of Roberto, with the understanding that it would be a need I filled but not that un-need I felt with Roberto, that spiritual ecstasy of love.

Is it damning of me to say that it was not peace I sought but drama? Does that only make me a schoolgirl? Isn't drama the highest art of our civilization? And isn't mimesis the function of both language and art? And isn't mimesis predicated on the other, brought into being through argument, through lying and making up and making up create re-uses for.

Creative re-uses for relationships. For bodies and their aftermaths.

What is the logic of menopause?

It is the logic of the longer human identity, *idem et idem*, because the Higgs Boson is Kali and it is decaying, radioactive living isotope of love, with a decay rate I can feel inside my womb—

Sasha

When I was fourteen I fucked a construction worker who was working on an office park opposite my subdivision, a young man of twenty-five or so but he seemed old to me then, and though Roberto had nothing in common with him physically, Roberto reminded me of him because they were both so innocent.

Even at fourteen I was less innocent than they.

Every article I've ever written I have signed over to Roberto as my penance. And they're not very good articles really. The ones Roberto writes are usually much better. But I give him an edge through sheer variety of volume of publication, his ghost writer and his toy.

As he likes to call me.

I am not a toy but I am silent like a toy, and I pliable like a toy, and I am patient like a toy, watching from the shelf, for the child to enter the room . . .

- -

I remember better than Roberto. I remember where we came from. And I remember where we are now.

Roberto is in a mental institution. And I am in Las Vegas.

But these are only physical places. And we are joined in places that are not merely physical.

I have faith, or hope anyway, that those places where we continue to exist together will be made manifest again, and that Roberto will free himself from Jerusalem, as I have.

I will always be a Jew but I have stopped being so stubborn. And if Roberto would only realize, that he's so close to being too stubborn to live, then I believe he could come back, come back to us, and see the great and terrible changes he has wrought, and see the beauty that is his inheritance.

Roberto has a child. One I am helping now to raise. Chiefly by scolding its mother, and I am good at that, but also with my faith, not a religious one but a human one, that this petty drama I have helped to stir up will have as its natural comeuppance a better future for us all—

I remember one of Roberto's poems, in my dreams, one I never remember when I awake, only how it makes me feel, with electricity over all my thighs, and a tightness in my breathe, like a headache coming on, and a light from the sky, meteorite—

- -

My Jerusalem is a city of scholars, and we keep the warriors close by. My Jerusalem is a city of light, impenetrable intoxicating light, and light's children, people, men and women.

My Jerusalem is a mad city and a free one, a little nest that I helped build with Roberto when he was offered a job at the Academy shortly after California broke off from the mainland it shortly thereafter declared its independence.

My Jerusalem is so afraid, so afraid that its mysticism, which is fragile, might be shattered, and it is for that reason that I collaborated in the summoning of the Door to Chai-Murry, because I believed we needed an anti-quark to our breakaway quark, to hold us whole and hearty in this strange world, and I still believe I was right, but as with so many fateful decision in human affairs, there is the Law of Unintended Consequences.

Perhaps we might say that that the Law of Unintended Consequences is the Law of Consequences Which Others, Largely Unknown, Intend upon us, and that's fair enough, but it's all a great unknown, isn't it, and so I was forced like we all are forced to simply wait and see what next.

What next.

My Jerusalem is like those first living cells amidst the clay of Earth, which created through their unique chemistry a semi permeable barrier in those bubbles of floating clay, the original cellular membrane, a shield wall that storms may yet come over, like electricity over the mind, the city is a mind, our own, but we do not possess it, it possesses us, greater ever day, for only recently are we come to cities, and we know now through archaeology that our coming to cities was for religious reasons, that they grew out of the temples, and our priests' ritual sacrifices therein, so frequent and abundant were they that cities became necessary to support our priestly class, there in Turkey, 9,000 years ago, before wheat, before agriculture, our temples of the dead rose down to map,

For that is what religion is, a map, and though cartography as a product of the Enlightenment is predicated or appears to be predicated upon a rational understanding of the world, Reason and Religion are two aspects of this greater face of human society which we are only now starting to stretch, as a baby, this truth we cannot speak, or cannot describe, but which we can map, as the deaf mute maps out for Hamlet the tracing course of his father's poisoning, I will map for you the dissolution of my marriage and the logic of our breaking away from your reality, because that is why you are listening, I know, you want to know how it was for the rebels.

For the heretics.

For all innovation is heresy.

And all stories are revolutions.

Roberto

And though I am coming, it will be silent.

And though I am resolved, it is unnecessary, because it will happen anyway.

Tell me now what you are seeing--

(Kex)

THIS IS A TEST OF YOUR EMERGENCY BROADCAST SYSTEM.

ARE YOU READING ME?

GOOD.

THINGS ARE ABOUT TO GET INTERESTING.

(Kex)

DO YOU REALIZE THE KIND OF SHIT YOU ARE IN?

YOU THINK YOU CAN JUST . . . WHAT IS IT YOU DID AGAIN?

Roberto

Above the Academy, all life has come to an abrupt pause.

(Kex)

I AM NOT COMPLAINING; NOT EXACTLY. IT ISN'T
AS I WOULD HAVE WANTED IT; I HAD MORE
HOPE FOR INTERDIMENSIONAL COOPERATION. I
HAD MORE HOPE FOR A DRAMA ON THE SCALE
OF DESTINY. BUT YOU OPTED FOR A MORE PETTY
COURSE, AND PERHAPS I CAN SEE WHY. YOU'RE
HUNGRY. I KNOW, YOU WANT BLOOD. AND
EXPLOSIONS. AND HEARTACHE. AND DEATH,
LOTS OF THAT.

I'M NOT COMPLAINING. I'M EXPLAINING.

THINGS HAVE CONSEQUENCES.

THIS IS ONE OF THEM.

Roberto

Everything that I could have been for you is gone; but I am
still with you, Sasha, even now, even now in this nuthouse I
am with you and I am stronger than you, because I
remember you even though it happened in a different
universe.

If I am awake then I love you. And if I am dead I love you. And if I am under a truck, crying, I love you, and if I am a freak I love you. And if I am straight as an arrow and vote Republican I love you, and if I am anything I am with you, forever as light—

--

Sasha

He forces me to speak. As he forced so many things. So many things for so many years. His libido, his desires, his needs, his horror, that I knew about. His horror of life.

He forces me to speak. I don't want to speak now. Let me go, Roberto. Let me go away--

--

Roberto

Sasha?

--

Sasha

Roberto. Let me go. Let me go, Roberto. Let me go.

- -

Roberto

Sasha?

--

Sasha

What is it.

--

Roberto

Sasha what time is it?

--

Sasha

It's time to get up, Roberto.

The Garden

I was turning under the light, and holding her hand,
watching the branches. All the light, an engulfment, bowed
me to her, piteously, harbinger of what is happening to me
now, a bowing before powers greater than my own, and a
break with all the laws that I had known.

Of course, just a pretty summer day, just a clearing in the
forest. Though not for me.

She held me knowing, I think, that something had broken in
me, something I would not get again. But I knew what she
didn't: the quarks were listening.

Quarks are listening inside the night, Muster Mark, doing
their pall and pull to unity we cannot but crave under our
eaves, fevered in our naked bodies sunlight and strange,
dimpled and dappled and set against the afternoon, the meat
for the cage of history, more beautiful than anything—

Sasha eviscerated me. She felled me and worked me to tell
me *what* so I could tell her *when* and we made a garden of
our minds without shame, after I'd had her, and she'd had
me.

A city may not be possessed, it is its own, even when
destroyed its spirit will not be possessed, the emergent
property of stones and planks and tar and brains of people,
whirring underneath the skies limitlessly, and so we made
our map of a city, an imaginary city, like a child that we
would not have, a vessel for our need.

Not long after we moved to Eidon. And renounced our
American citizenship, to become Californians.

- -

162

I am a professor but I can no longer profess what I believe because its time is not yet come; like Copernicus I must leave it to a protégé, one who is yet to arrive, and therefore, perhaps, all this knowledge of mine may simply pass away, it is not needed, it will come again in a different form, to someone else, knowledge works that way, it is never one's own, never for a moment, not the first moment and not the last, it is shared, secretly, under the bones of the earth, inside the quark's trembling grace our communities accept what they must when they must and never before . . .

- -

I must get back to her.

I must prove that I was right; that despite everything I am stronger than Sasha thinks, strong enough to throw off the cloak my own imagination has forced upon me, to insist I can greet the consequences of my decisions on my own terms; that I can escape the nuthouse.

That I can go back through the gate . . .

Roberto

Tell me and I will come, wherever you are I will come,
again and again, to you, my love, though it be my death,
which it will be—

Tell me where you'll be, though I can't come, and I will
come, under the pact of stars, by your dream, inside your
mind, under the thought, redeemed after mountains
crumble, an ecstasy of the beyond brought close, closer,
within you like my soul—

Tell me now so I can speak your name into your ear, to
remind us both just what the hell that name is, what the
sound and what the pause and which this sibilance to insist
I'm yours—

Tell me when and tell me where and tell me why and I'll
tell you the season and the secret and the meaning and the
inlet by your raft under your skin where I came in that last
night we were together, like a shiver when I was a ghost—

Tell me it's you that I am true to, that the feeling in my
head is you.

Tell me that the feeling in my head is you, that this quark is
yours, stretched uncountable perturbable perambulated
musical excusable fruitier than tutus the quark broad and
deep, ribald and creepy but sleepy too, the quark brought
out and wrapped about us like the night, wherever we both
are, apart—

Tell me that you're there inside my head and that I'm there inside of yours, a power and a grace without a scourge, only a limitless horizon dreamt instantly and silently for one moment before it's rushed to hospital to eat its final course—

Tell me that I'll get out Sasha.

Tell me that I'll be yours again.

- -

Let me die. And let me die. And let me die, though I cannot. And let me die, though I shall be with you, and it will be horrible and horrifying, let me die, and I shall be with you, and we shall get to the bottom of this horrible muck, as though to drink its last dregs, and imbue our bodies with its muck-flesh, stronger than anything we've ever known, the piss after eating the grapes of wrath.

Let me die, so that I will see you alive, where you are, where you are coming, where you are come, naked, and desirable, and fruitful at last, your womb, your womb, your womb,

A Volga.

- -

Let me die. Let it come over me, the shackles of the surrey, with the fringe on top, to bear me eastward, steady eastward, to your lair, in your mind, on fire, your secret lair, like Batman's, under your left frontal lobe, egregious and mad, and fertile, let me die and go there to your brain, to speak with the immigrants who are arrived there, inside your brain, like Jews, after the Holocaust, unbeatable, near dead, almost dead, unkillable, more beautiful than ever, defeated, indefatigable, filled with revenge, unable to speak, filled with poetry, filled with more poetry, pissing grapes of wrath and unguents of accord untranslated but nearing a sense of meaning, through facial expression, and body language, a physical comedy of the now, your immigrants are coming now, and I will die, to come to your brain to greet these brain-immigrants, these cerebral Jews, come into your frontal lobe to make music, and eat pickles, and assess the situation of situations, Chai-Murry and its octagons, Grim Castle and its ostriches, Ancestral Gate and its ragamuffins, and me, me and my academic worries about the size of my balls, I am come to be made into the weapon you need, iron transmitted by quark, into your head:

I am arriving.

MY NAME IS SASHA

I am arriving in your head

MY NAME IS SASHA

Sasha do you hear me?

MY NAME IS SASHA

Sasha is it you?

MY NAME IS SASHA

Sasha, what is it?

I FEEL A FUNERAL IN MY BRAIN

Whose is it Sasha?

I FEEL A FUNERAL IN MY BRAIN

O—

A FUNERAL FOR YOU

The City is Destroyed

The city murders even in its death, Los Angeles.

The Volga is come.

"What did you think you were doing?" Sasha asks.

And I tell her, everything: Sasha this is an attempt to make
sense of things but it must be more so instead let me say,
this is how things make sense now: I am walking, as under a
breeze, and I am feeling, a certain energy, and I realize, the
city I am walking in is already dead, though it doesn't look
dead, and I realize, that I am in a kind of ghost city, LA
perhaps after the Nuclear Holocaust, but sublimated into a
subliminal vibration, on the edge of hearing, running over
my nerves, I am walking, towards Sunset, north, passing the
bike shop, passing the boat stop, passing the rye bread seller,
approaching the book store on Sunset, the pavement and
the sky, I am broken already, I see that, but not as broken as
Los Angeles. Sasha, it's like this: you made it, I know you
did, but this is the aftermath, whatever you did, and I know
that it was you, you changed everything, and I can't get it
back, maybe you can get it back but I can't, and so this is all
that I can do now, keep going though I know I've lost. But
life is losing, the most beautiful thing is that truth, that life
is losing, and every loss is more beautiful, I believe that,
Sasha, and now I am approaching the bus, small god, bus
god, we need a god of the bus, what can we name him, or
her, let's name him Bovgorod, the Bus God, I see his ape
face and hair, meaty, full of pain and energy, like a cloak, or
a gill mouth, lubricating my entrance to the bus, the god's
mouth swallows me, and I am aboard, inside the dead city I
am aboard Eklaihah, which is Dead LA, Eklaihah, a hollow
shell, a horror of such beauty that I know I will never leave,
at least, never leave the same:

The orange trees are blooming over the streets of Los Angeles after the nuclear disaster and I am keeping your locket next to my chest as I approach my grave, as I approach the wolf who will take me the crow, as I approach Echo Park above downtown I am a busrider and I strike up a conversation in my approaching death The Now my approaching death The Now and my approaching death The Now my Sasha can you hear me, can you hear me Sasha, tell me can you feel his face against your breast, it's bus god, it's Bovgorod, the mighty bus god, and he is driving east, along Sunset Boulevard, and the rattling of our cage and the balancing act of my feet and the grin of Bovgorod's avatar, the bus driver, he is Rastafarian, or a recovering Rastafarian who is learning to accept the gays, as perhaps Vladimir Putin will, now that he has nuked LA, and come to Echo Park, my Echo of your York, my echo of your Yew Tree with my iron in my head, I am the echo of your yew Tree with my iron in my head, coming now to you, Sasha, you immigrant, you brain, you terrible Volga, I am riding on the bus god to your apartment in the Manhattan of the west, the dead island, the huge vortex, under the shadow of Dodger stadium, my brothers, in arms, I am a wastrel I am falling, I am falling into you over these dead pavements, tell me, Bovgorod, what is the sweetest thing about being a god of buses?

You're asking me?

Yes.

*it's like this, asshole, I ram all reams and I kill all dreams
before they're born because I prefer dreamless sleep aboard my
buses because aboard the bus we can learn at last how to kill,
how to kill the right way, we do it silently and without
weapons, and we do it with love, with the power of the poor,
we commune in the brightest of daylight, In the brightest of
nuclear daylight, my servants commune a beauteous motion
round their Beltane, this little fire, my autobus, this vehicle of
my love, this sentence of the divine comedy, bearing east,
marking twain, marking twain on the sunset, hold my hand,
Roberto—*

I hold the bus driver's hand as we approach the Volga
coming over us, over the dead city, after the neutron bomb,
the ecstasy of tears, and the flood of the Russian river, into
the steppes of the Manhattan of Los Angeles, echo park, the
gentlemen's game of hell, over my boot soles, Sasha:

The bus stops under the trees and I get out.

The lonely sound of wind warms my gut, my upgraded gut.
And I remember:

Well, never mind what I remember, Sasha.

I am bearing east, towards the wolf.

I am bearing east, through dead Los Angeles that is
Eklaihah, I am bearing east, over Sunset, on foot, the bus has
broken down, and Bovgorod is chanting, with the help of
his avatar, the bus driver, chanting on the sidewalk next to
the bus shelter, I am walking, over the bullet holes of
Rampart Station, I am moving east, towards the hill and the
valley, passing Walgreens, on the north side of the street,
moving east, bearing eastwards, as Ing did, up the Volga,
towards Russia, and towards death, the dead city makes
music for me with its dead lips, a music that is: ash and
broken ash and stream and thunder, thunder in your belly,
thunder in your belly, Roberto, in your Intelligent Upgraded
Gut, the rumbling belly of thunder and the rumbling
thunder in your belly, let us meet the dead, and let us meet
the many dead, so that you may meet the wolf too, because
you had to know, you had to know, and so let us know, and
let us all know, and let us all know all manner of things, and
let us know all manner of horrible things, forever, and ever,
amen, amen, amen, amen, and I am coming now upon the
bodies and the corpses, living corpses, yes, they're zombies,
it's a zombie apocalypse, and there's a lot of revelations
coming, except they're nice zombies, and basically they're
just dead people who are alive, and I know you know what
I mean, Sasha, because you've been like a dead person who's
alive for a really long fucking time, and the corpses rose
from the street.

Five bodies in their tattered post-nuclear clothing like Mad Max or Journey to the Center of the Earth, I can still hear Bovgorod chanting with his avatar, trying to get the bus to start, but eastwards where I'm standing on the broken sidewalk the corpses unfold the card table and spread over it a tablecloth and pour their delicacy of fine blood orange tea, from Orange County, so beautiful and fragrant, and they speak with two voices, and the first voice comes from three of the corpses at once, and that voice is named Lucifer, and the second voice comes from the remaining two corpses, and that voice is named Mary, and Lucifer and Mary and I sit down to Blood Orange Tea in Dead LA Eklaihah, which happened during my journey towards the wolf, who would bring me to the crow, so I can reach your brain, Sasha, and come to know you, and come to be with you, and come home at last, inside your brain.

> LUCIFER
> God art with me, and I am a fire. How do you do!
>
> MARY
> I'm Mary
>
> ROBERTO
> I know I should recognize you or something but I don't. Who are you?

LUCIFER
This is my city and I am light. I am all photons and
all tragedies. I bring you peace and I bring you war.
And I bring you my hand, here, I'll detach it now,
for it is your hand, now, Roberto, I'm giving you
Lucifer's hand, my hand, so you can bring light into
the dark places, and so that you can bear my mark,
like Cain, and know that you must bring light, for
you are light's servant, and Los Angeles makes
movies because of the light, and because of the light
I love you, Roberto, though I am only a dead
zombie.

And I take the zombie's dead hand, shining with enormous
green fire, and put it in my pocket, and I promise, I promise
Sasha! I promise I will show you the dead green zombie
hand, if it is the last thing that I do, because I love you, but
more than that, I am necessary, and so are you, and if this is
coming through to you, know that it's twitching and
glowing in my pocket right now, just waiting to hold your
hand.

They are beautiful and dead and my city is beautiful and
dead and I come because of what I did. I am come because
of what I did, I am come because of what I did, and the
zombies and humming, they are humming over the tea, and
the hummingbirds come in, buzzing over our table, to get
the orange blossoms, and the city is alive.

The city is alive but the humans are dead, and it's just me
and the bus god and some of these avatars, bearing east,
bearing east, but tea isn't over yet:

LUCIFER
I like Los Angeles. It helps me think.

173

MARY
Well, the place is named after me. I guess I like it.

ROBERTO
Really, it's named after you?

MARY
Yeah, that's me, "Queen of the Angels," ha ha ha.

ROBERTO
I didn't know that.

LUCIFER
You don't know much.

ROBERTO
Well, that's true.

LUCIFER
Let me tell you how little you know. When I was a boy I could take the red trolley to the Pacific Ocean for a nickel, all the way from downtown LA to the ocean, because things were more democratic then, and because I was just a boy. But all beauty must die so new beauty can be made, and I accept that. I accept that you're an ignorant fool and I'm just a dead zombie Angelino named Lucifer, bringer of light in dark places, sometime filmmaker, sometime pornographer, lover of women and men and children, one of the undead, tell me, Roberto, is it true you come from another dimension?

ROBERTO
I don't know, man. I don't know where I come from. Do you know?

MARY
I know, Roberto.

ROBERTO
Where?

MARY
I'm a breeze. And I'm singing on that breeze. That's where you come from, Roberto. That breeze that I'm singing on.

ROBERTO
I don't understand.

MARY
Well maybe you will someday. It's okay to not understand. Only human, and all that.

And Lucifer, his three zombies, and Mary, her two zombies, they stand up and finish their tea, and they salute me, with a little irony, and with a little pride, and I bow to them, and I continue my journey east, along Sunset Boulevard, along the Path of the Wolf, towards El Sereno, and towards Pasadena, where Philip Marlowe comes from.

Is the dead city alive? It's Sasha, I know that now, she did this to me. Her and Kex. She cheated on me with Kex and so all this occurred, because they couldn't have a nice normal discreet affair, it had to be all occult and shit, all fucking Kabbalistic, and because of their goddamned lust, and because of their goddamned obsessions with Spooky Ass shit, and because of my own goddamn obsession with Spooky Ass shit, we've left the universe we knew behind, and I am a little Motie in God's Third Eye, swimming through the aqueous humor towards a star system I can almost make out. . . in El Sereno . . .

I am forgetting. And forgetting is beautiful. Forgetting is like the blossoming of the orange trees, and the spraying of graffiti over the sidewalk and over the cement walls. Forgetting is like the rebirth of cities, who in their amnesia give birth to wondrous things, whole philosophies.

I'm witnessing a whole philosophy being born, and I don't even know what it is, just that it feels like forgetting, like I'm finally slotting myself into place, like one of those cute little glowing cubes slotted into HAL's brain in *2001*, slotted into place, kept in the drawer with justice and beauty like the professor in *It...* starring Malcolm Macdowell, one of the best films to come out of the 1960s, and in my dead city which is your dead city named Los Angeles Eklaihah, one of the roughs, dead suburb of a dead daydream, unquenchable thirst for the steppes of Russia a Volga of Tenebrous Embraces made Pure and Noble by the calm of the moment before the Earthquake, and I feel Charlton Heston's shadow hovering over me, beautiful and serene, and I shout into the sky a word I've never heard before, the syllables relaxing my throat, for this dead city is mine and it is beautiful more beautiful than any living city it is a voice, my voice, and I am its, and in this hungering birth I slap the sidewalk Philip Marlow towards El Sereno, into El Sereno, past the cheap motels and into the mental institution.

For my mental institution has no bars. and it is in the suburbs.

And it a lightning rod and it is a justice, but it's not where I'm headed, I'm leaving it behind, bound for Pasadena, over the open road, under the oak trees, I am shouting at the sky, the clouds are like my face, untranslatable, but felt in the medulla, my heart, O my heart Sasha, when will I reach you?

(after you meet the wolf and the crow, Roberto)

Right. That's right.

The City is Destroyed and it is justice and I am content and unafraid and the heat is rising slowly over the sidewalk, shimmering.

The Wolf is sitting outside her home, smoking a cigarette on this hot day, though she shouldn't, just like she shouldn't be watering her lawn in these summer months but she does it anyway, she does it anyway.

"Wolf, is that you?" I shout, and she beckons me over, cigarette in hand, and I'm afraid, I'm afraid to step over into her vestibule, not because I know what it will mean, but because I don't, because it could mean anything, because old women are crazy, and this old woman is The Wolf, and she could eat me alive, or blow my house down, or show me how to reach the Crow, my friend, and so I step over the threshold like Gilgamesh through the Gate, and I realize now who I am, I remember.

I remember the pain and I remember the journey and it's not important that I describe it because I know where I'm going.

Into the future.

And that's where you're going too, I know that.

But Sasha, she's not going into the future any more. Because she's dead. Because I killed her. For what she did.

But not yet.

I'm not going to kill her yet.

Because sexual violence is not permitted in Disney rated movies which is what this is, it's a literary novel made for Disney with a lot of science fiction in it, and a little theater, well, you know exactly what it is, you're holding it in your hand, or you're transmitting it into your hippocampus, whichever reading format you prefer.

Sasha, are you there?

(I'm here, Roberto)

I love you.

(I know)

- -

I know I love you but this has gone far enough. Because male adultery is permitted and female adultery is not, that's just how the cookie crumbles, because women love war and men hate it, and that's just how the cookie crumbles, because we made it so, and because we made it so, and because all manner of people made it so, over the fiery divide of history, over the torturous path of consciousness, into dreamworlds and back again, and into dreamworlds and never back again, I will not excuse my behavior, perhaps because my behavior needs no excuse, or perhaps because there is no excuse for it, or perhaps because excusing behavior is tedious, and changes nothing, and I bear east to the Crow (but not yet)

O, not yet.

For the Wolf shall tell me tales, and so shall you.

And one is that I outdrew a swan at a pencil contest (maybe I'll tell you that one later), and one is that I died (I'll definitely tell you that one), and one is that I grew to appreciate Kex's sense of humor about the whole thing.

Kex was stronger and smarter and richer and better than me and that's why I hated him, and that's why I fucked him in the ass, because he was gay and I wasn't, and because the Academy isn't fair and because my research wasn't going well.

I killed Sasha in Las Vegas.

I keep my coed there.

With our daughter.

My son, Alice.

With my tomb.

With my conscience.

With my irony.

With my sword.

My sword named Ing.

And one story I especially remember from the Wolf's lips was this one:

"I was running in the grass and I smelled it overhead, the crow, bird of prey, bird of estuaries of cement, and I wanted it to tell me, who I was. Because Crows know, who people are. And so I asked it, Crow, who am I? And it told me, you are the wolf. And then I remembered. And I howled into the concrete sky in Pasadena back in 1971 when the skies were always the color of concrete and I dreamt of Philip Marlow every night, as I lay beside his fire, telling my children tales of the Fiery Wood, like the one that goes

" 'The fiery wood is great and bright, burning in the daytime of the night, and all of you who're fast and fair, shall be buried there, under the sun of dark, when all is lost and broken on the thorn, I keep under my foot, to howl with: ' "

My children have left me. But I am a crone of Wolf and this gives me special powers, Roberto. Do you fear me?

"Yes, Wolf."

"What have you brought me so I don't have to hurt you?"

"I have brought you my wife's head"

(And the stars are falling, Roberto, the stars are falling, tell me, will you, where I died, will you tell me where I died because I don't remember dying and I don't remember where it was and I so want to know, I want to know just where it is, can you tell me?)

Shut up, Sasha.

- -

I left the Wolf, feasting on my wife's head, and bore north, to downtown Pasadena, home of the crow.

What is it to cohere? Is it to stick together, like clay? Is it to stick apart, like nails and boards? Is it to fly apart, as words do?

And if something is comprehensible is it coherent? And if something is just, is it beautiful? And if a murder is cruel, is it better than a murder that is cold?

I don't know. But I am coming closer to my goal, of publishing my magnum opus, The Great Adventures of Roberto and his Many Animal Friends, brought to you by Several Big Jews in New York, or, its alternate title is, A MAP OF KEX'S FACE, and What Was Found Therein After the Cartographer Had Gone Mad.

I'm mad. Mad in the dining room.

Let me tell you the next part of the story now.

The Crow of Pasadena

Crows are secretive because they have been many places,
and know many languages. In their travels they have
absorbed the meaning of places, and so have come to know
the conceit of place itself, which is that it exists, though it
does not. Crows know that places do not exist, only people,
and as with all things, it's both what and who you know,
and Crows are compiling an index of both, inside their
shared mind, an index I dream of sometimes when I am
high on opium, and one I daydream of sometimes when I
am sobbing in the shower, and my little daughter Alice is
pounding on the door. I can hear her voice but I can see
their great sublimated index, splitting like vast sentence
diagrams, behind my eyes.

Why did I marry a woman I knew to be infertile?

I know it was because I did not want children and did not
want to admit that to myself.

Though she did have the one abortion.

The Crow of Pasadena lives above the bank and so I fire my
trusty grappling hook up onto the gargoyles and slowly
work my way up the molding, towards his eyrie.

Pasadena is beautiful when it's dead.

I am done with mapmaking.

Here there be dragons, baby.

Dragons forevermore.

- -

The Crow of Pasadena is like a small dragon, almost as big as a medium sized dog, its beak big enough for a policeman to carry it as a bludgeon.

Its eyes, like Hyperion's, meditate horribly upon the state of matter and its dissolution, and I, sweating, untie my grappling hook from the gargoyle and —

And suddenly I remember that you wanted me to kill you. That that's why I did it. Though I wanted to do it too.

"Which is more important?" asks the Crow.

"They're both important."

"But which is more?"

"I don't know."

"Neither do I."

The Crow flutters its wings.

I watch the Crow's eyes, and know that it's telling me something more, something I should be able to understand, if only I were smarter, or more psychic, I should be able to say, just what it is, just who is coming, just what I am becoming, just who it is that I must meet, to take me back, to my young family, to Sasha's corpse, to Vegas, and the Magical Isle of California . . .

"Where do I go now, Crow?" I ask, but He flaps his wings into the air, and sails into Pasadena, over dead dark Pasadena and the lights go out with the Crow, for he is the God of this place, and shadows magnify and dance inside my eyes, and the Spiders are laughing in the doorway, and broken yellow light, lances of yellow colored light are screaming over my eyes inside the dark and the city is crying, the city is screaming, Pasadena is screaming for its mother Marlow, the Marsh Bottom, the Horselover, Philip, where are you, Philip, Philip, where are you?

Over the darkness I can hear the Crow's wings, and I can hear myself vomit on that Pasadena roof.

There is no recovery and there is no excuse.

But there is truth and I seek that still, even without my map, even with only part of my memory.

We are possibilities. And I am transmitting Sasha as I am transmitting you, as you are transmitting me, we are light.

We are eternal.

But which signal goes to which place, or to what who?

What who am I, broken, working but broken, mad.

Mad early is mad late, and I can slow my mad, if not for this damned sky, because the Crow rules, and so I must climb down in the dark, without my grappling hook, down the gargoyles faces and limbs over the facade of the bank, down into the darkness of Nightmare Pasadena.

- -

I have abandoned my map and so can't depend on its soothingness, the knowledge that borders exist and they can define me.

The black and starless sky trembles over my body like a shroud that I can feel it talking to me, words fragrant alien and divine, not heard with my ears but felt under my skin, electric impulses meaningless and comforting as dawn light in the darkness, the empty Pasadena skyscrapers sad and monolithic grays against the infinite black.

"I'll kill you again, Sasha!" I shout into the darkness. Though I won't.

Red light not dawn but Kex is shimmering ahead. Kex is red and humorless, atrophied and stretching rosy-fingered over the dead Los Angeles sky, just you, Kex:

"Why are you named Kex anyway!" I shout into the creeping redness, energy from galactic center, pale opaque and velvet not sky but bodily fluid, not blood but serum, a drug, some part of Kex murky and hidden, selfish and honorable, desiring, hedonistic murderous ecstatic urge and urge, enveloping the night:

I took Kex because he was a nobleman and though I would have killed him so many times, to fuck him was to relive me of the need for killing, a smaller justice to stand in for the bigger one, unfulfilled.

"What now Kex!" I shout into the red.

What good does it do to kill the unfaithful wife. She was infertile anyway; it isn't as though I'm preventing the birth of children not my own. Only my ego. But which part.

Which part of me was responsible for the murder.

I have to get back.

"I have to get back, Kex!"

The red, amoeba-like, trembles over the sky, clasping the dark like the edge of a screen, for what are we imprisoned in this warm drum, beating all our hearts against the screen, hoping it will hold out the dark, hoping it will keep out the dark, what we will never want to learn, the vastnesses too cold for effort or reason, implacable spectacular intrusive horrible because it isn't us and we might have it be, as some have tried, as I have tried,

Should you greet the darkness?

"Should I greet the darkness Kex?"

I have so many times. Like Faust. But I never made a specific bargain I only started conversations, but isn't conversation also a bargain, in this prison of language, the dance and bow of counter point and edge implied and middling exacting its costs, insisting that once begun it's never ended—

You have to pray, Roberto.

I hate praying.

I know.

"What are you doing to me Kex!" I shout into the sky.

What did you do to me.

- -

I know I shouldn't.

Just tell me that I shouldn't.

Tell me that I should go back to it all, go back to my ordinary life, back to my insane wife, back to Israel, or back to God, or back to California, just tell me that I should go back, that I should climb the Castle and fling myself off, that I should die rather than go further away, that I should—

But on I go.

Deeper in to the puzzle that makes me a man, and makes you, well, whatever you are.

What are you?

I'm so afraid of you.

Do you have powers I don't have?

Do you make music in the morning?

Have you gone into these strange places and forgotten things?

Have you been here?

Is it some failing in my character?

Am I blessed and cursed with some charade that I can barely perceive?

Is this life my only life, or have I had others?

What does it mean?

- -

I want to burn my maps, burn my software, burn away the part of my brain that insists on mapping, comparing, ordinating, applying scales and matrices and models, but I know that if I were to kill that part of my brain so much else would be lost with it, my sense of self, my sense of irony, my will in the world.

My will in the world is onwards, but this means that I can't sum or solve or save these problems I have helped create; they're bigger than me now, probably always were.

Deeper in—

Have you been here?

Tell me:

The walls stretch far away, like vertical plazas, revealing this space that's like being at the bottom of a big stone box with angled sides, thick lush wet stones and trickling light from far above, an oubliette, which means forget, and that's just what I want to do, I want to forget.

It's what I wanted.

Adventure.

Well, now I've got one.

- -

The Castle speaks to me, in my dreams, saying:

We knew what you were fighting for. Your own death. That's what you wanted all along, so we decided: we need a little blood. If the guy wants to die so bad, let him do it on our stones. We could use a little snack. So come on in big guy, this battle you are gonna win...

A doorway opens in the oubliette revealing a passage further up and I take it, moving up the steps, around the sides of the oubliette, moving up. The light is charismatic; that is, it lends a spirit to the place, almost hopeful, it's true and washed and tricky underneath, and I'm stepping, one foot in front of the other—

The ghost of Sasha climbs onto my back, her hands vipers bent into my shoulders, I shall carry her forever, but I don't always feel her.

"How does it feel, lover boy?" she whispers in my ear, but I don't answer her.

I'm going up, up to see the sunrise, though I know that there can be no escaping this forgetting.

California is the imagination, and it is the prize, one we cannot utter, nor frame, like the holiest of holiest, it exists only in the mind of God, and in our own, secreted away—

"I'm gonna laugh when you're dead," says Sasha on my back.

"I know," I say, and climb faster.

I cannot jettison her but I can jettison myself; only my body will remain. Only this biped body, without a name and without a history save that which is written into my flesh, the history of all mammals, inescapable but open to interpretation—

189

I am climbing.

I can feel the sun above, and I know that this is a secret sun. For this is a secret world.

And I am a secret man, bearing my secret dead wife on my shoulders. "Secret" is related to a root for "separate" and so in this sense is like judgment, though it is a private judgment. What one on one's own says now shall be, what shall the reckoning be, when there are no others around to say, or when they will not speak, or cannot know that it is their right to speak and so say nothing.

In the secret I will find the secret, the secret of secrets, and if I do not I know I will forget even my body, and even my wife's body, and here split many times, from the American mainland, from quotidian society, from secular society, from the planet Earth, from my dimension, from my marriage, from my friendship and my love for Kex, from my own sanity, and from my oaths and promises, split all, separated secret, I meditate within this Castle in the California of my Californias, unknowable but one which will be translated, for after all I'm telling you about it:

What I needed to find . . .

Up into the sun with my dead wife on my shoulders I submit to the authority of The Castle, but only for a moment, only for this moment, as I rise into the sun, out of the stone stairwell, winding out of the oubliette and then up the final steps into the field, the field that is another castle, wider than this earth.

For reality is a system of castles, if you like, gates and barriers set by lords and governors and their lieutenants, demarcating these boundaries and subjugating our realities to the frames of our senses, in whatever capacity best serves these powers, and in whatever capacity we also choose.

"Isn't it beautiful, Sasha?" I ask.

"I hate you," she whispers.

Four, like the doors in the door out of Chai-Murry, these four Towers which are more Spirals of Stone than Towers reach above me, surrounding me in the field.

The sun is brighter than anything I've ever seen, illuminating every blade of grass, warming my face.

The Castle is a whole World, and I must climb into its heart . . . but which way?

"Which way, Sasha?"

"That way," she says, and points at one of the stairwells winding upwards into the sky like a filament of steel spun out from a bridge of unimaginable immensity, starlight—

I step in.

And this climbing is something else, a rendering to an entryway, I feel heat in my body and there are no longer stairs, I feel myself shift, I feel space shift around me, I feel myself flying, and Sasha is laughing in my mind as her ghost laughs upon my back and a part of me has never been happier, knowing that this too, is possible.

This, too, is possible. And if I am to return, in any way imaginable, I must decide what it is that I want to return to.

For all my crimes, they still exist.

And I know this is only a whiling away the hours until the Po Po shows up, or the executioner ...

But maybe not!

This corrupt world may have any number of things in store for one such as me, and I will just find out. We can always use another murderer, can't we?

Can't we always find room for another murderer!

- -

Inside me I can feel the Crow, and his Grace. The Grace of the Crow is like the Grace of God, so deep that you don't want to know, just how it works, but you know you could, if you really wanted.

The Crow is accessible even as he is divine, and he moves over my face in my sleep, my dreaming sleep, to show me just where it is I need to go—

Sasha is dead beside me.

"Sasha, wake up!" I tell her.

She has bled to death.

She rolls over, her neck flopping a little from where I gashed it open.

"Morning already?" she says.

- -

I know that The Castle is also Kex's Head, and so as I climb within its recesses I am working deeper into the mind of my old friend.

What does this mean? Kex was instrumental in the arrangement which split California from the mainland; both physically, and politically. He initiated many of the most important ceremonies; the beginning ceremonies. Like the Big Bang; most of what we can do now is just try to puzzle out what happened in that first instant, and reason out the laws that have come to be because of that irrational and arbitrary set of coincidences resolved then at the beginning of the Universe.

The Castle will be mapped, I know, I will map it, I will map Kex's head even as I undertook to map his face, because it is something that I do, though I don't especially want to do it, it will happen anyway.

But why map it?

To show the way for others, of course.

The most dangerous thing of all.

To seek out the demons, and then tell your friends: they're this way.

Demons up ahead.

This way lie dragons . . .

Abandon all hope, all ye, all of ye, my fateful few, my lovers and friends, abandon all hope, for it is Reason which will guide you through this course, through Hell and beyond it—

Flying

I am flying; I am the The Crow.

Over the city of the Castle, much like the Academy, but more recursive, an M.C Escher framework spinning charmingly down into the green spring California hills . . .

This world of mine; this world we have made.

I am like a god, but this is what all men have thought, I know. All men who stumble on a secret, all men who make some new and powerful tool; they think . . . God has spoken. God has shown me the way.

I Crow, I a U_2 instrument aloft, a drone, a weapon.

I have just this moment . . . just this moment of freedom. I must relish the air upon my face, and relish the knowledge that I have nothing to do but eat some bugs and return to my nest . . . and meditate on the forces of the universe, of course, what Crows excel at, but before I go, I want to know the Crow's name, my own name, what is it?

What am I called?

I'm falling . . .

The Castle

I can feel Sasha in Las Vegas, pulling the handles of the slot machines.

I'm sorry I killed you Sasha.

I'm sorry about that.

"I know," she whispers, the flutter of the corpse about my ears . . .

I will go into the Castle (though I am already inside) because it is my duty, I know I must do my best to chart this course, I must join our universes, not with something paltry like the little door but with something large, like a Universal Law, or the coming of a God . . . or the sound of a Crow . . .

Something I must make or find to join this broken people and these broken worlds . . .

I will be sacrificed, of course, that is what often happens to the men who decide to throw themselves into the breach at the crucial moment . . . but not always . . .

I am moving in space, the heat passing through my body, and I know that I am slipping into Kex's antechamber. Into his room above campus, his hideaway, where he and his dog could play, where he and I once made love.

One of terrible truths of the head is that it is a thing of predators. The eyes, nose, teeth and ears of the head are so made to predate better, to arrange the body for some good eating.

So to map this Castle is to map the logic of predation; that is, of eating, by force, particular things that one wants, as an organism. Some lifeforms take what is given them, what stumbles into their mouths, and some take it, and mammals and birds and so many other things, we with heads, have decided we're interested in taking it . . .

Yes, the head is, if not the root of intention, the master switch for carrying out the orders, the General, the Mighty General Encephalus, Mighty Encephalus the Stormy One, greater than Zeus and greater than Cronus, greater than Uranus even, Mighty Encephalus the General the *Strategos* who carries out the Will of the City, the means and the ways . . .

Yes, the Head, the Castle, is the Ways and Means and Committee, it is the routes and the avenues and it is the Orders and the Reasons and the Logics and the Knowledges and Memories all these for food into the mouth, and avoiding becoming someone else's meal . . .

Inside my head I am inside Kex's head, and my wife inside mine, though she be dead, though I be dying, this Castle will yield up the Way, I just need a little Way, just a little Northwest Passage, to show the Eager Young Explorers just how it's done, how does one break away and found one's own Little Universe, children?

(Or, having done it, how do you go back . . .)

Inside Kex's Antechamber Alice holds me from behind, her smooth skin pressed against my waist, her hands clutching my chest.

Like a bat-ghost Sasha's spirit flies away from me and out of the window, over this dark mirror of Campus . . . flying away . . .

Alice holds me in her huge and warm embrace.

"Alice . . . Alice, tell me. Which way is up?"

"I am," she says.

"Will you come back alive again, Sasha?"

"I'm Alice, Roberto."

"Oh, I'm Roberto."

"Yes. And I'm Alice. Do you see the city? Do you see what the city is doing for you?"

The people are waving their flags down in the plaza, the Great Bear, ursine and flatulent, resplendent on the rag aflame in their colorful hands, the people of my city, dreaming me, saluting me . . .

"They're afraid of you, Roberto. And they might kill you if you don't put them at ease. Go out, and speak to them."

She gives me a little push out onto the balcony, and as her hands push me out, and I cross the threshold, everything is gone.

Snow covers the universe. And I remember that I am the Human Crow, and that the winter is come, and that I must make haste into the horizon to find my mate, before she flies.

I board my motorcycle and light into the west, shrinking infinitesimally, west, and down, into my heart.

Tell me, Sasha, is it so with you?

Kex?

I'm dying; I know it.

I'm dying.

Tell me: when does it happen? I need time to prepare.

The buildings rush by me like old gods.

The people are flying in the air.

They're making music with me.

Remember where you're going, Crow Man?

I can feel Alice's fingers on my back . . .

The motorcycle can drive itself and I lower my head down to the handlebars and the speedometer and let the machine's vibrations sink into my skull, into my body, resuscitating some deep part of me . . .

Can it be a poison if it tastes so sweet? Abandon hope, all ye, and yet, it is the present.

With the future gone and hope with it, the present is even brighter.

See it shimmer over your face?

Time is coming closer to us.

Perhaps this is why I am writing this confession in the present tense. The future and the past have less meaning to me than they once did.

This terrible and oppressive now, this musical now, ecstatic, reasonable and hieratic, unnamed and unnamable, altruistic and afraid, my heart—

Sasha, do you forgive me?

Over the snow I ride, my token of a body to this storm my city state created but which I am a part of, I am guilty along with all the dreamers, all those goddamned Spanish dreamers who picked up that fucking novel, looking for the map, the map to the Promised Land, and found instead some lover's soul, and his dream kingdom of an island and its map, but no man is an island but every man is an island and I am climbing, Kex, I climb the mushroom kingdom of your brain, my fellow encephalopod, for though my hands are angry they are kind, and I accelerate into the turn, and I will bring you with me, I will bring you with me—

Over the skies the snowflakes are like gods too, but everything is gods, a trillion tiny ones so universal and so temporary, just decide, Roberto.

That is the function of the brain, that is the function of narrative, that is the function of love, decide, *jetzt oder nicht*, and *jetzt, jetzt ist:*

Color.

It will be color.

Red, of course.

Simply because.

And in my soul I feel the choir calling, of the color of my blood, and the color of your dress.

And the color of your thought.

And the color of my hat over this burnt world, inside the castle of your head, Kex, I just needed that little trinket, just that little trinket . . .

I dive into a thousand oubliettes, my consciousness a hernia in some vast organism's bowels, because enlightenment is just a glimpse, and then you are returned—

Returned

I am spat out by the fountain.

Covered in shit.

The police arrest me.

Now for the trial of my crimes.

In the jail shower I am healed, for the world is still here, and I can still hear Alice's voice inside my head, or is it Sasha's . . .

And the motorcycle in my hands, and the slot machine's lever in my fingers . . . but that was Sasha . . .

The guard scans my bar-coded wrist and we prepare for sleep, the jailbirds whistling to one another like crows to mark the passing of the dark hours inside the institution . . .

- -

I am a murderer, but murderers are useful.

In our new state, all bodies are needed.

That is the great crime, from the admittedly somewhat evil perspective of the state, of murder: you took one of us away, and we need all of us. And we need you too. Plus, you're useful. You're a killer.

Let us foment your rage, killer.

Let us put the tool in your hands.

Killer, be with us. Killer, be for us. Killer, are you for us?

Tell us, beauty, what is the nature of your murder and what is the nature of your god, and are we at harmony in our thoughts of blood and lust, and will our deeds or crimes be examined and will they be remembered and is now the time, and is now the time, for us to greet this day with our swords?

I am sleeping in the California jail.

My woman's voice inside my head, all of my days. All of my days my woman's voice, inside my head, all of my days.

Until Kex comes to visit.

Until I tell him about the red.

About the color that I found inside his head.

The color that can save us.

Red.

In Class

"What is a facial expression? And what is the duration of it?"

The room is silent. We have no windows. Like a Sartre meditation.

Koony, my favorite student, speaks:

"You killed your wife, Professor."

Red

Writing and thinking are decisions, every moment of every thought, and every ordering of every word. The logos is holy because all language is in a sense prescriptive; as we describe, so may it become, if it is not so already. So we dance with the universe, lying and telling it the truth so as to receive the same in return . . . what I wanted, and what I got, was a democratic mechanism to link these strange worlds we have tumbled into, and are still tumbling into.

And I thought, why not let it be a color?

The simplest of passwords, and the deepest of moods, an undulating fabric of our thoughts, it will change red of course, for now every red will be more fraught, a gate, every time—

Red and red and red.

Just put it on and think it; and we are away.

I've made California red, but there will be other colors.

I am a murderer but I have my daughter.

And my mistress.

And you, shall you build a state?

Welcome us in, eh?

Tell us what color to wear.

Epilogue

There are so many explanations for so many things but I feel obligated to affix here some of them in the interests of *the what ifs*, and *the what came afters*, as every Lord of the Rings needs its Silmarillion, as every *Ulysses* needs its ranting wife, as every Yossarian needs the new horizon, this ocean, this time, when no one will be shooting at him . . .

I have abandoned my profession.

As I have abandoned my city.

I moved to Vegas where my mistress insists on living, with her hologram experiments.

Vegas law, like California's, is forgiving of murderers, fresh from the jaws of revolution as we are.

Why did I kill my wife?

Disgust, I think. Simple disgust. But do the reasons matter? It's something that I did. What if I said I did it out of love, not to make her suffer any more? A nonsensical answer, but then, life is always suffering, isn't it, and so we could have any kind of sophistry we wanted, it will not explain anything.

No, I see that epilogues are in fact not the place for explanations at all.

They're footnotes.

For small stories that append. Or branch off.

- -

My daughter is named Alice.

Like so many names, the name Alice means "noble" because everyone wants to be noble, even in a democracy, everyone wants to be noble.

When Alice is five, I will bring her to the California border, and give her a red T-shirt.

And then she will know that she can go any where she wants . . . and then come back.

The Germans have been experimenting with green . . . but it's been many years since I've been to Germany.

Mapmaking is changing. I can no longer make much sense of it; it's too much like psychology for my taste, and I prefer my woman to do my headshrinking if it must be done.

The eye apparently evolved to see only blue and green, since those are the only two colors which can penetrate water. So it is remarkable, in a way, that we can see red at all.

One reasonable theory is that we evolved the ability to see it for berry picking.

And I like this theory because our expanding Neighbor Universes are like these berries, for the picking . . .

That's what red does now, you see? Makes all the novels real . . . but now you can get back. Some novels thousands of people live in, millions of people . . . and some only a few.

They're all out there, just waiting, all those trillion universes: you just have to want to visit.

With my days now, I try to do as little as possible. Political considerations are fortunate for me, in that I am a valued diplomat from the California Republic and can exist with my small family (modestly) on the Vegas state dime.

Would the explanations make you feel better, if I offered them? Most explanations are lies; or, at best, fabrications with the ring of truth, but no factual basis.

The facts are these: I am a Californian. I live in Las Vegas. I killed my wife. I have a daughter. And for a time, I went away. And then I came back. And I brought with me a map, so that others might go where I went.

It's not a very reliable map.

Who is Kex, you ask?

I hardly know.

Some worship him. Some want him dead.

He's an important man. And he made a decision, like I made a decision: to open our borders.

Like the Cambrian Explosion opened the borders of the design of life, 500 million years ago.

Life in a myriad of colors forms on such decisions, terrifying and absolute, rich terminous and strange, for I know, like Kex does, that this decision will bring with it the inevitable extinction event, that so many of these doors we have flung open will, perhaps soon, be closed forever.

But such colors till then! When Sasha wore red for the first time, I almost wept, she was so beautiful . . .

ABOUT THE AUTHOR

Robin Wyatt Dunn was born in 1979 and lives in Southern California. You can find him online at www.robindunn.com. You can email him at settdigger@gmail.com.